THE DOLL PRINCESS

THE DOLL PRINCESS

TOM BENN

JONATHAN CAPE
LONDON

Published by Jonathan Cape 2012

2 4 6 8 10 9 7 5 3 1

First published in Great Britain in 2012 by
Jonathan Cape
Random House, 20 Vauxhall Bridge Road,
London SW1V 2SA

www.vintage-books.co.uk

Addresses for companies within The Random House Group Limited
can be found at:
www.randomhouse.co.uk/offices.htm

The Random House Group Limited Reg. No. 954009

A CIP catalogue record for this book is available from the British Library

ISBN 9780224093507

The Random   Council
(FSC®)   Our
books carry   LEWISHAM   is the
only for   LIBRARY SERVICE   ntal
organi   cy

Types   d,

For Dad

The saga begins, beget war . . .

Mobb Deep

1

THE KING

July 1996

SOMEBODY ONCE TOLD me that before prison, Frank
used to moonlight as an Elvis impersonator. Rumours
can be dangerous things.

I watched two new lads go in first for a bollocking. I
pulled up a stool, took a reckless sip of Styrofoam-cup
tea and opened out the *Manchester Evening News*. Tea
rings, biro scribble. The paper was torn, missing half a
headline. I looked at the bird that had made the front
page.

My top lip was burning.

She had olive-skin, sharp features, and was well put
together – tallish, maybe. Off-the-shoulder sweater.
Short black pencil skirt. Unforgiving heels. Lips sucking

what could've been champagne through a thin white straw.

I lifted the *Evening News* up to show our Gordon. He was sat at the corner end of Frank's marble-effect bar, reading today's *Mirror*.

'What you make o that?' I went.

'Fuck me. Better than in ere, that.'

'A nine or a ten?'

'Ten. Aye, that's a ten.'

'Thought she'd be too dark for you,' I said.

'Not arsed, me.'

I laughed. Gordon thumbed back the *Mirror* – big hands making a noisy mess of the paper until he was near the front. He spread the pages along the bar, ironed the creases out with his arm – held it up for me.

'Nowt t'write ome about that, is it?' Gordon was snapping the topless blondie from behind the page with his finger, making her tan-bed legs and belly wobble. He shook his head at me and then went: 'Sayin our standards are too igh, mate?'

'I'm sayin you wouldn't kick her outta bed, neither.'

'Pends,' he said.

'Depends on what, mate?'

'Pends on if she brought that ten along wiv er.'

Gordon flipped his paper over to finish reading the sport.

I went back to the ten on the *Evening News*. I recognised the surroundings – she'd been snapped in Terence Formby's Kitchen Club just down the road, and recently, since the decor matched their refurb job last May.

I lifted the paper off the bar so the Pole could give the place a once-over before opening time. I left the picture alone for a minute and began reading the story:

Twenty-three-year-old Egyptian-born student, model and socialite Saafiya 'Safir' Hassan was found dead yesterday morning in the basement of a Manchester block of flats. The cause of death is unclear, with reports of heavy toxins in Safir's bloodstream, neck injuries and strong evidence of sexual assault.

Belgian-schooled in her teens, Safir was the heiress to the growing multimillion-pound Egyptian Hassan oil and export fortune. She divided her British life between London and Manchester while studying Law and Business at Manchester University. She was last seen leaving the exclusive Kitchen Club on Deansgate with an entourage in the early hours of Wednesday morning. Police are hunting corporate diplomat Abdul Muhsi, who vanished shortly before her body was found. Muhsi is believed to have functioned as her British chaperone and is thought to still be in the UK. Safir's partially clothed body was discovered hidden underneath rubble . . . [Contd. on page three]

I turned over, put the *Evening News* back down on the bar. The page corners became a damp see-thru grey that glued poor Safir face down, smothering her in disinfectant. I skimmed the rest of the article, feeling like shit, and gave my tea another go.

I burnt my bottom lip.

The Pole was trying to finish off the bar. He was an illegal, all Frank ever seemed to hire. Our Gordon rubbed his boxer nose as he read – sniffed, yawned. The Pole cleaned round him. Gordon didn't look up.

The empty restaurant tables out front were cut into daft shapes, all laid out in a slick jigsaw pattern. *The Britton provides opulent urban dining*, Frank once paid this poncy food critic to write in a local rag.

I looked at the clock on the wall and then breezed through the *Evening News* again – still bomb stuff, more bomb stuff – stopping on page nineteen. There was a fifty-word piece in the bottom-right corner, no picture, squashed next to a big colour ad for double-glazing:

> *An investigation is under way into the torture and murder of a twenty-five-year-old prostitute identified as Alice Louise Willows. Her body was found dumped along Stockport Road near the McVitie's factory on Wednesday morning. Police are following up a lead on a black or dark-blue BMW, possibly a 7-Series, with private registration. They are appealing for further information.*

I went to school with an Alice Louise Willows. She lived down the road from me in Woodhouse Park when I was a kiddie. Her mam made gingerbread and all sorts and used to say I was a good lad for walking with her girl to school. In fact, Alice Willows was the second bird I ever shagged and should have been grateful she hadn't been the first. I hadn't seen Alice in a decade and it felt like more. But she'd be twenty-five now. It was her and she'd ended up on the game. Tortured. Murdered. Fuck.

I looked up then over my shoulder as Bill and Ben came round from the back, went under the bar – started for the door.

'Your go,' one of these young lads said to me as they headed out – face screwed up like a toddler with a scuffed knee.

'Is fuckin chef in yet?' Gordon shouted to them as they left, still nose-down in *the Mirror*.

'What's up with you?' I said. I got off my stool to head into the back for my go with Frank.

'Not ad me Weetabix,' Gordon said, folding up his paper.

I looked at the clock again. It had gone half noon.

He said: 'Could do wiv summat when fuckin staff get in.'

Frank Holland had a thick brassy voice. Thick short arms and legs and a rugby-ball-shaped face that wrinkled when he was happy and wrinkled even more when he wasn't. He had bad Elvis mutton chops and a Brylcreem quiff, which led to some of the lads calling him 'the King' behind his back. He was still on the right side of fifty but he'd have to show his passport to get it believed. He'd only done the bird the once – a short spell for a Section 20 before I knew him. These days he was a posh city-centre restaurateur, loan shark for five area codes and a small-time but steady ecstasy distributor. We all helped out. I'd chuck veg in a pan, kick in front doors round Openshaw and run small traffick and supply on a weekend. I was young but they came younger. Besides, I'd fucking earned my spurs.

'Ah told um both. Ah said "nobody sells in these clubs but us. Yav three fuckin venues ter cover, three fuckin venues! Two nights a week. Yer not exactly stretched fuckin thin." Ah said "It's agreed. That's yer turf, that's where yer surf. Now fuck off."' Frank bellowed this to me across the table, exploding in laughter. 'Bastard kids playin silly buggers. They can all piss off.'

I reached into my Harrington – took out an envelope and pushed it towards him. He'd just put away a large fry-up.

Frank said: 'Least ah can always rely on you, Bane.'

'Six ton,' I said.

'Fell out of is pocket in the end did it?'

'Aye. On his way down the stairs.'

Frank laughed. Frank brushed through the wad of notes with his thumb, a yellow thumbnail that needed cutting – speeding up the job. 'Thought ee dint av owt? Spose to av cut off is benefits along wiv is bollocks.'

'Says he won the other night at Belle Vue.'

'Fuck off. Six hundred quid? Oo was the lucky dog?'

'Him,' I said.

Frank laughed again. I waited until he'd finished.

'Frank, you know owt about that prozzy killed the other night? They found her up on Stockport Road.'

'Where'd yer hear this?' he said.

'Read today's *Evenin News*?' It was folded up crisp on the table, next to his empty plate.

'Ad a quick look.'

'In there.'

'What, she a little friend o yours was she?' he said.

Little Alice Willows. Poor cow.

'No,' I said.

'Yer busy tonight?' he said.

'Might go out for a drink with n old school mate. Why? You need summat doin?'

Frank grinned. 'Nah, don't go mad on the Dandelion n Burdock, son.' Frank frowned. 'Jus pop round the Chemist if ee rings but that's bout it.' He pushed up his cuff and squinted down at his Omega. 'Are we fuckin openin ere or what? Where's me staff?'

I twisted round and saw our Gordon coming through into the back room. 'Anythin goin?' he said.

'Fuck off, big lad,' Frank went. 'Get ter bloody work.'

Gordon eyed up the remains of the King's fry-up. 'Oo made that?'

'Frank did,' said Frank, patting his flab. 'A right belly-burster.'

I stood up and zipped my Harrington.

'Tell us a dirty joke, Gordon,' ordered the King.

I looked at them both. Gordon opened his gob and then shut it again.

'No?' Frank went.

'. . . plus rohypnol equals yes.'

Frank roared.

* * *

7

I came back through to the front and the Pole tossed me a wave. Posh surfaces buffed up a treat. My Styrofoam brew was still on the bar top so I picked it up, put it to my lips and tipped. Cold.

2

CAST STREET

I WATCHED HER scuttle across the Red Beret car park
towards me.

'Bloody ell,' she said, 'look at *you*, ay? Look at yer!
Gorgeous.' Her white heels clip-clopped faster as she
got nearer. She gave me a squeeze by the doorway.
There was strength in it.

Jan Dodds was now a curvy five-three, cropped dyed
black hair with a nice bit of rack on show courtesy of
Wonderbra. Her fresh face was pancaked over and her
tired brown eyes were quick and pretty.

She'd worn well enough. It had to be almost ten
years since I'd seen her. She pushed her right cheek
up to my lips and I gave it another kiss.

'It's bin, God, ah dunno – donkeys!'

'Drink?' I said.

'First one's on me, enry.'

'Oh aye?'

She walked through the pub doors, grinning up at me, warm hand squeezing mine – no ring on her finger. 'Expectin some scrubber was yer? Bet yer was, n all.'

'Nah. You're lookin fab,' I said.

'N you enry. So what yer avin?'

'I tend to go by the family name now, love.'

'What – Bane?'

'That's right.'

'Jus Bane?'

'Yeah,' I said.

Jan showed me her teeth. 'Alright, lovey. Whatever yer say.'

We sat down in an empty corner booth and I watched her get through a packet of B&H and a few Aspalls. I listened as she told me about how well she was doing. Part-time receptionist at the Health Centre . . . recently single by choice . . . thinking about starting night classes . . . house of her own on Footman Avenue . . . There was even more go in her after a couple of vodka & Sprites. I'd give her a question and she'd sit back – take a second to mull it over – eyes going, dead giddy. But then she asked how my old man was getting on:

'No idea,' I said.

And then we got round to it.

'You eard bout it then?' Jan said.

'Yeah. Saw it in the locals,' I said.

'Can't believe it, me. Poor bloody Alice. Jus can't believe it.'

'Did you know she was on the game?'

Jan's eyes narrowed. 'God, yeah.'

'You were still knockin about with her? Weren't you two joined at the hip in school?'

'Mates, yeah – but nowt like you n er were back then.'

'We were never like that, me n Alice,' I said.

'Yeah, well – she were livin in Wythie still at one point. But then she moved all of a sudden. Saw er in town the once. Adn't seen er since las Christmus. She were jus wanderin about on er bill. Bane, honest to God, right, she looked terrible. Like a different person. This were – must've bin like May, early June time.'

'Before the bombin?'

'Yeah.'

'She'd been at it awhile, then,' I said.

'Ah reckon, yeah. But ah dunno. Ah dunno anythin, me. Ah dunno ow anyone gets in that state. Or bout what's gunna appen wiv the funeral n all that. Poor bloody Alice. God. Ah still can't believe it yer know? Murdered. Ah miss them days. School discos n skivin off.'

'Do you?'

'Don't *you*?' Jan bit her bottom lip.

I looked away.

This young lad got up from his seat, came past the bar and the busy magic-eye wallpaper and went over to the jukebox. He fished through his change, ran his finger down the lists and shouted out:

11

'Bastard. Got any Blur on this thing?'

'Get fucked!' someone said.

He put a coin in and sat back down.

Happy Mondays on the go.

'Appy?' Jukebox Larry, still shouting.

'Get fucked!'

I walked our Jan back. Her ankles a bit shaky in those white stilettos.

It had just gone midnight when we came out to the car park. The night was dry, warm, missing a breeze. She had hold of me by the arm, stiff fingers, gripped to go.

'. . . yer copped off wiv er, enry bloody Bane – she bloody ate yer bloody face. To the last song n all – it were – what were it now? Oh yeah – 'There Is a Light That Never Goes Out'. Ah were dead fuckin jealous, me. Ah wunt speak to yer on our street fer time. Member all that?'

'I hated that fuckin Morrissey,' I said.

'Ah fancied yer. God, it seems dead daft tellin yer this now.'

'Soppy bugger. Daffodils? Fuck off.'

Jan shrieked with laughter.

We got to her road but seemed to be carrying on.

'Thought you said you lived on Footman Avenue?' I said.

'Ay? Ah do, lovey. Well – jus off there. Our ouse is on corner o Cast Street.'

Cast Street? That street was fucking rough. Two long rows, both sides – odds and evens – as bad as each other. The crack addicts, the squatters, the pub-barred dossers. It gave fair Wythie a bad name. Council seemed to have declared it a write-off. In the last couple of years it'd become its own grubby little commune.

After five minutes we crossed over the road and Jan stretched out an arm and pointed at a house.

'This your gaff then?'

'Yeah, thas it – thas the one,' she said. Her voice had gone all sweet and quiet.

The front gate stuttered open and we made it to the step. I put my hand up her skirt as she fiddled about in her purse for her keys. She closed her thighs on my fingers for a second – let go and said: 'Bane, behave!'

Inside the house. It stank of gas heating, dirty plates. The hallway was cluttered with Littlewoods cardboard boxes, heaps of clothes on the carpet and stairs, catalogues piled up underneath the phone table.

There was a German Shepherd dozing under a radiator. She popped her big head up when she saw me, whining *hello*. Jan shushed her with baby-talk.

A telly was on loud in the front room. The light from the set was glowing between the door and frame.

I said: 'Not done too bad then.'

'We know it's not too swish, right. But it's fine fer us, honest – it does the job, like. It's jus what we need fer time bein.'

I shut the front door. Jan put her keys and purse down on the phone table, then came back over and started on my shirt buttons.

'Off! Get it bloody off!' she giggled.

'Our turn to get it now is it?'

She nodded, kissed me a couple of times – soft, sticky – then her lips pressed harder.

The telly in the front room got louder. Jan ripped her lips from my neck and turned her head. 'Trenton? Trenton! Turn that pissin telly down! Answer yer mam!'

'Fuck off!' A voice from the front room, muffled, like the gob the voice belonged to was full of scran.

'Right. Right thas it.' Jan's eyes went wide. Her hands left me and she was gunning for the front room, still wobbly with the drink. 'Yer little bastard! Don't yer dare fuckin speak tuz like that.'

I buttoned my shirt and followed, pushing the door wider. 'How old's he?'

'Ee's eleven,' she spat.

'Forgot you had a kid.'

He was sat on a big dog-mauled sofa chair. Biscuit crumbs all over the show. She'd left the little man in the house all night with a packet of custard creams and the telly remote.

'Well say ello then,' Jan said.

'Iya,' he said to me. Eyes on the telly.

'Am waitin,' Jan said.

'What?!' he went.

'Down. Now.'

The telly volume went down.

'Ta.'

Jan took my arm and led me back into the hall. 'God, am dead sorry bout that.'

'Bet he's a good lad in the main.'

She said: 'Anyway, lovey – where'd we get to?' Eyes small, mouth wide.

I got dragged up the stairs and pushed in the back bedroom. I switched the big light on but she switched it off again and turned on a little frilly lamp near the bed. The room was painted white undercoat and from what I could see, a damn sight tidier than the downstairs. She had a low double bed, purple duvet, white pillows, a cracked mirrored wardrobe, a bedside table and not a lot else. There was a faint scratching sound coming from above us. I looked at the ceiling – heard a couple of soft thuds.

Jan shut the door behind me, snatched her earrings off – one then the other – and tossed them onto the table. She pulled her black tank top over her head and chucked it away. She dragged her knickers down and stepped out of them ungracefully, skirt and one heel still on. It was all there, ready and waiting – and she stopped and blinked at me, breathing herself horny. I started to get undressed.

We made it to the bed. She rushed her tongue over my chest, tracing wet circles, her body bouncing on me, hands all fidgety. I tugged her bra straps down, scooped a decent handful of tit out of a padded red cup.

A thud came from above. Then another.

I said: 'What's that racket?'

Another thud.

'Ay? Oh, don't mither bout that – jus them rats up in loft.' Fingers attacked my belt buckle – gave up – had a go at my fly.

'They're some big bloody rats.'

I looked up. She carried on.

I said: 'They must run along the row. Bet they've all got um round here.'

'. . . yeah . . .'

'You wanna ring council.' I said it to the ceiling.

We got it done. My mind wasn't on the job, though – Jan kept apologising every time she called me Henry, bless her. And there was that poor kiddie downstairs.

Afterwards she sat up in bed and watched me get dressed.

'Bane?'

'What, love?'

'Nowt.'

'Y'alright?'

'Me? Yeah. Ay, d'yer want some weed? Av got some weed in the drawer if yer fancy it? Mean – yer don't av to but—'

'I'm good, love.'

'Sure?' she said. 'Jus a puff?'

'I'm right, me. I'm gunna get off now.'

'Then ah think al jus roll up a little one. That's if yer don't mind, lovey.' Giggling, she kicked back the duvet – rolled half out of bed to reach the drawer, tits swinging.

I watched her get out her weed bag and a skin and start rolling up a fat one. 'Jus fuck it!' she said, laughing. 'Ah mean fuck it – why not? A quick joint now n then'll do yer no arm.'

I said: 'You sure you're alright, Jan?'

'Me? Yeah. Yeah, am grand, me. It's jus maybe things are a bit shit right now. Av jus bin thinkin bout it all, yeah? Trenton off school is doin me fuckin ed in. What appened to poor Alice. God! Everythin. Am alright. Am alright, though. They're jus a bit shit. Things. Shit. Everythin at the minute.'

'That Health Centre payin you enough?' I said.

'. . . Actually . . . av not got job yet. But – right – interview fer it's tomorra n am gunna get that job, Bane. Honest to fuckin God. Am jus tryin so ard at the minute.'

I took my wallet out and dropped a fifty onto her bedside table. 'Ee-ah,' I said, 'Get them rats out the roof.'

'Oh Bane, love. Don't be daft. Yer don't need to do that.' She reached for her lighter.

'What time tomorrow?' I said.

'Ay?'

'Time's your job interview tomorrow? Mornin?'

She nodded before lighting up – said it through her teeth: 'Quarter t'nine.'

3

DECENT RAP MUSIC

NO JOY WITH Jan. So little Alice was on the game, we'd established that. Jan didn't know anything – she was busy in her own mess, like the rest of us – had been for a while. But maybe I wouldn't mind helping.

I had a late lunch at Frank's and drove out to Stretford to pay the Chemist a visit. Gordon was collecting money on foot while it was dry. He'd do a sweep of the pubs, bookies and a couple of unlucky homes. Gordon liked playing the hard man anytime, anywhere. At the footy stand or in town – he took pleasure in all-round terrorising. I said I'd pick him up outside the old cinema afterwards, if he could be mithered to stroll down that far.

I parked up, got out and knocked on the back door three times. Stark opened up and let me inside. There was a white dust mask hanging under his chin, elastic string behind his big daft ears. 'Alright, Bane?' he said.

'Yeah, good. You?'

'Not bad, mate.'

We went into the front room. It was brown and spare. There was a couple of Fosters cans on the floorboards, one more in Stark's hand. A ragged edition of the *Radio Times* was poking out of a pond-coloured sofa – cushion like a ham slice. But the room had no telly.

'After a brew?' Stark went.

I was tempted.

'No, ta,' I said.

He raised his can, shook it.

I shook my head. 'Any trouble?'

'Nah. Quiet. See the game?' He tipped the dregs down his throat.

'Missed it. Is he up in the lab?' My finger pointed up.

'Im? Oh aye, yeah. Always workin.'

I went up the stairs first, Stark behind me, a fresh can in his hand from the crates they kept in the washroom.

The swampy boom-bap bass of decent rap music was blasting out of the lab. I pushed the paint-stripped door – knocked hard on it after the fact. The Chemist waved me in with his back to me. He was busy pissing about with the scales.

There were plants growing along the counters, most of them dying with the fumes – but they had too many to fit in the spare room. A portable telly was on mute, propped up on a workbench, a foreign porno playing in the VCR. Drug dust everywhere. A copy of Shulgin's *PiHKAL* and a cassette-stereo balanced on the window-sill, caked in whizz. You could scrape five grams off the speaker tops alone.

Stark followed me in.

'Leave the door open,' I said. The fumes were too much for my lungs.

Organized Konfusion gave in to a Mobb Deep tune. I went to the stereo and turned it down. The Chemist finished up and came over.

A daft curly mop of mousey ginger hair and a bum-fluff beard gave him that air of brainy student scum. He was twenty-odd, old enough to know where the barbershop was, but he just wouldn't be told. He was also rake thin. He hated getting pulled up about either.

'Get that fuckin hair cut,' I said, pulling the elastic of his dust mask and letting it snap back over his gob.

'Dick ed! No need.' He took the mask away and rubbed his face.

Stark had put his mask back on. 'Yer don't wanna be breathin this shit in all day, mate. Wacky fumes. Send yer doolally.'

'How've you been, then?' I said to the Chemist.

'Busy. Busy – Busy. You?'

'Weren't you spose to give our Frank a page?'

'Bane. I've not got nowt fer yer. Want an excuse or d'yer wanna know where else yer can get some decent honest gear fer Friday?' His scrawny Adam's apple bounced as he spoke.

'It is Friday,' I said.

'Exactly.'

'Well?'

'Go see Maggie,' the Chem said, 'Down Otterburn Close. The Fold.'

'The Witch? Otterburn Close? You're askin us to trek down to Otterburn fuckin Close?'

'Yeah. Flat fourteen C.'

'What's your game, son? Fobbin off your biggest pay cheque – pushin it into someone else's pocket cos you can't be arsed to work your trade. Hangover is it?'

'I'm not fobbin yer off. I'm tellin yer – av not got it. If yer must know, av jus found out I've lost me weekend. Got a mate comin up t'stay from—'

'Fuck off.'

'Look, the Witch int competition. It's not like she's runnin a serious operation. It's the Mad fuckin Atter's tea party down there. No seriously, I'm surprised nobody's wound up bloody dead.'

'You're really sellin this to me now, son.'

'No. Look, yull be right. Yull be made up. Bloody ell, call er a mad cow but from what I know Maggie's not sloppy. That cow knows exactly what she's doin n she keeps it tickin over tidy in her own way up on Planet Allowe'en. She dunt buy off the gypos down there – she sells it off to um. The rest of it, pills n that, they come to her to trade n she dunt buy any shite. She makes jus what she needs – the ome-grown psychedelics, erbal blends, the lot – jus enough to keep the whole ouse appy – sorted – nuffin big time.'

21

'Not like you, Scarface.' I ran my hand through the plant leaves growing under the lamps.

'Fuck off, smart arse. N ow long's it bin since yuv seen us wiv coke?'

I walked over to a rack of test tubes on the next sideboard. 'So?' I said, 'Better off with the minor jollies than to aspire for the rest o the pie. Step on toes in that sink and you've got yourself problems.'

'But they respect the Fold down there,' the Chemist went. 'It's fuckin hallowed ground to them lot. She dunt av security fer that flat or owt.' He nudged his head towards Stark. 'They protect each other, look out fer thy fellow neighbour n all that. Real sense o community.'

'I'll tell her you said we could have a discount for the inconvenience.'

'Why do yer celebrate in causin us grief? Can't yer see I'm up to me fuckin eyes in it?'

'She's gettin the extra business,' I said.

He made a fist, poked himself in the eye with a knuckle, itched his beard. '. . . She probly will let yer. I dunno, ask nice. Don't – look, jus don't displace the ouse vibe. Yuv seen what they do to foxes down there?'

'Foxes?'

'Foxes. Yeah. Like dogs but they bugger wiv yer bins.'

I rolled a test tube off the counter. It smashed on the floorboards like my old man's good china.

4

MUSHROOMS

'Otterburn Close?' Gordon said to me in the car. 'Fuckin rough round there now, Bane. Bloody ell.'

'Why do you think you're mindin the car while I go in?' I said, slowing down at the lights.

'Bastard.'

We carried on to Hulme. An afternoon job was becoming an evening job but the light was still strong.

'You get anythin done?' I said.

'Nowt really. Thev all got a story ant they? N they can all do wiv a slap. Mind you – ah got the interest fer that car the Johnstons bought fer their girl. Kids on the street av already let the pissin tyres down. Shame.'

'How much did you get?'

'The full grand.'

'Was sir in?' I said.

'Was ee bollocks. Wish ee ad bin. Nah – jus the missus.'

'You didn't.'

'Ah did.'

'You didn't. N the cash?'

'Well she ad it dint she? She were game. She ad it all to give.' Gordon was lying. He took out the notes, opened up the glovebox and pushed them inside without making room.

We were nearly there.

'Dint they find that dead bird ere the uva day?' Gordon said.

'What, mate?'

'It was on news. Yer know. The ten. That Paki model or summat.'

'Egyptian.'

'Aye. That were it.'

'Was that *here*?' I said. 'They found her body in Otterburn Close?'

'Ah reckon. Yeah.'

I turned onto Bonsall Street. 'You might be right.'

Gordon said: 'Disgustin that. Gorgeous thing she were. Only young.'

PIGS GET THE FUCK OUT

. . . read the big orange letters sprayed on the back wall of the courtyard.

The flats were low-rise and made a big, mad

chessboard. Graffiti stopped the pattern. Skinny deck access, water damage, burnt-out caravans, barking dogs, jungle anthems on nicked stereos, Yardies, gypos, eleven-year-olds with Stanley knives, students, mountains of worthless shit everywhere.

The bullring and surrounding crescents had already bit the bullet. Or in their case the wrecking ball. This would too, but not soon enough.

I parked up and got out.

'Shan't be too long,' I said.

'Best fuckin not be,' Gordon said, switching my radio on.

I'd never visited the Fold but I'd heard the stories. Crack den like no other. Why they called Maggie 'the Witch'.

I took the stairwell up one floor, dodging broken needles – walked the deck until I found the right door. My ear against the key-scratched wood: a dub tune throbbing from inside. I kicked the bottom of the door twice and listened again. There was a wait. Then the door opened a gap. It was on a thick brass chain and underneath that was the face of a small white boy – nine or so – gazing up at me. I couldn't think of what to say. We stared each other out for about ten seconds and then he pushed the door shut. Chain-rattle. The door opened again fully.

The boy had gone.

This was my welcome to the Fold.

I counted seven in the main room, half-hidden in

the stinking haze, dossing about on the carpet and sofa chairs, enjoying the quality poisons. Some were watching an episode of 'Countdown' on a large colour telly but you couldn't hear Whiteley over the music.

The wallpaper had been torn down and replaced with activist slogans, big hippy posters, newspaper cut-outs, daft graffiti. I noticed a blue budgie in a dome cage in the corner when it started tweeting along with the music.

There was a prozzy sat with a bloke on one of the sofas. He was busy toking on the strong stuff, calling her names in between steady puffs. He wore a tatty Fila jacket and paint-stained 501s. She was all legs, few bruises.

I made my way across the room.

The pimp started shaking his Bic like a maraca.

'Easy, soldier,' the prozzy went, reaching out to stroke his close bowl-cut.

He gave her the salute, screwed up the burnt foil and chucked it at her. She turned the other cheek and clocked me as I passed.

'Alright?' She smiled — followed me with her eyes. She was young and pretty and bony.

I nodded and passed by, stepping over two friends of Dorothy cuddling up on the floor.

There was this Jamaican old-timer in a tan safari suit sat on a chair on this side of the room. Next to him was a closed door. I could see a bald head under his leather flat-cap. I touched the walking stick by his leg and he looked up.

'Maggie,' I said, 'She in there, yeah?'

'Sidung, ya earz-hard – ya be nuh bad mon.'

'I don't think she knows I'm here, pal,' I said.

He laughed from his belly. 'Jah know.'

'Some bloody kid let us in.'

'Sidung. Jah know.'

Behind me there was even a white Rasta, annoying the budgie now – dancing round its cage, poking his fingers between the bars.

I unzipped my Harrington and sat on the floor. I could see better from down here, just below the cloud.

The pimp was still smoking hard over on the couch – grey cheeks sucked in. His face looked like a polished skull. Other than him and his stunning merchandise, everybody else was a supermarket vegetable, a month past their sell-by.

I waited.

The Jamaican tapped his cane.

Carol Vorderman showed us her sums.

After a couple of minutes the door next to the Jamaican opened and the young lad who'd let me in the flat poked his head out.

'Come inside,' he said. No accent.

The pimp coughed. 'Ee-ah. It's our fuckin turn. This twat jus got ere!'

'Shud it, Den. Jus leave it, yeh. Jus shud it,' his bird said, clawing at his wrist as he tried to stand up.

He belted her away and went: 'You shut the fuck up you or al give yer summat to whine about. Ah saw yer givin im the eyes yer cunt! Think ee'll fuckin pay fer—'

'Sit down,' she said.

The rest of the pasty locals watched on – soupy-eyed. None of them made a sound.

'Come inside,' the little boy said to me again, like nothing was about to kick off.

I got up and zipped my jacket.

'Ya blackheart, mon?' the Jamaican called out to the pimp. 'Tack-tack. Hah hah hah . . .' He shot the pimp a gold-toothed grin, pointed his hand out like a gun and flexed his trigger finger. 'Tack-tack.'

'Yer wanna get on our fuckin case, n all? Fuckin knock yer out . . .'

I left the Jamaican and his belly-laugh and followed the boy inside. I looked back just in time to see the pimp sitting down, the prozzy jump in his lap – fussing for him to be quiet. Then the boy shut the door.

'Welcome to my house,' Maggie said from behind the table.

This was the kitchen. It smelled even worse.

There was a giant crucifix hanging on the raw plaster wall. The daft ganja-scented candles on the table gave it all a grubby Dracula feel.

I said hello.

A fancy hookah in front of her had seen plenty of recent action.

The boy picked up an empty disinfectant sprayer off the sideboard, unscrewed the head and filled it with water from the sink.

'Does he belong to you?' I said, sitting down at the table before I was asked to.

'Jacob?' she said, 'Jacob belongs to this house.'

I watched him screw the top back on and water two plant pots on the dank windowsill. Daylight, just starting to fade – fat shadows eating the courtyard. Next he sprayed some little mushrooms that were growing inside the filthy cupboards and on the wall shelf. Afterwards, he picked some of them, ran them under the tap and put a couple on the table in front of Maggie. She sliced the tiny wet roots off herself with a kitchen knife.

'Try one,' she said to me.

Jacob perched himself up on the manky units – underneath the crucifix, his legs dangling. He watched. She dropped the biggest mushroom on my side of the table.

'No,' I said. 'I'm good.'

'It won't lie . . . they can only show you . . . truth.' The Witch was breathless between words.

'I'm not after magic mushrooms, love.'

Her matchstick arms and straw hair made her look a fright. She wore a skintight vest and the sultana skin of each arm was ruined – striped in bandages. She looked like she'd been left out in the Sahara for a month. Then pickled.

She said: 'This is . . . psychotropic harmony . . . positive power for confronting the mind. It's nothing to what's waiting . . . out there. What wants us . . . dead.'

'N what would that be?' I said.

'Burundanga,' she said. 'It . . . wants us all. The weak and the strong.'

'What's burundanga?'

'Burundanga is . . . very fucking dangerous.' Her leathery face split into a grin that did her no favours. She wasn't young.

She nudged the hookah to one side. There was a drip-stand and an oxygen tank waiting in the far corner of the room.

'That's very fuckin dangerous,' I said. 'There's a gas explosion in these holes every other week.'

'We know . . . we care . . . It's us who burn. But don't worry . . . Maggie is not the name of his latest flame.' She put a finger to her flat chest, 'The flames are here . . .' then moved it up to her temple, '. . . and here . . . Nowhere else today.'

'Not you I'm worried about,' I said. 'Or your house.'

'Everyone . . . respects . . . this house.'

'Wait till you see the twat out there. Who's he tryna impress?'

'He won't . . . visit us again. Look outside . . . we're at war . . . in here . . . they come to my house . . . to wash away the smell of death.'

'Don't you smell o death?'

'No. But you do, chief . . . You're in mourning. What can you smell in your dreams?'

I was bored already. 'Don't think I smell anythin, love.'

'What do you see in them?'

'Straight paths with trees either side. That's what I fuckin dream of.' I cleared my throat. Stopped pandering. 'Our usual supplier's gone tits up this month. I was told you could throw us some E at decent wholesale rate. We're lookin to spend maybe a grand. Maybe more. If you have that much and I like what I see here. Which I don't.'

She gave me that night-terror grin again. 'You're blunt for a new face. We have . . . what you need, chief. Tell us . . . your name.'

'Bane.'

'And who is . . . the *we*?'

I looked down at my watch. I saw the second hand flinch three times and then I looked up. 'So you have it, love? Nice one. Now what's the damage?'

'It's nineteen-ninety-six, Bane. And still they bomb us . . . we passed that corner . . . that they told us hell was around . . . I'll give you them for . . . a flag per Adam. How do *we* feel . . . about that?'

'Made up.' I showed her I had the cash.

'Jacob . . . reads . . . palms. He'll tell you your fortune. Now? No cost.'

'I thought the gypos were down there,' I said.

Jacob cracked a coffee-bean pot and took out some gear. He slid off the counter to hand it to her and she passed me the large clear vacuum-sealed bag. I split it and tapped a few into my hand. There was a ball of empty button bags tucked inside the big one.

'This is a good batch . . . one hundred . . . They're not cut with . . . aspirin . . .' she wheezed.

'Pure bloody aspirin more like. This'll be shockin.' I was pretty sure it was the good stuff.

'No,' she said. 'These are . . .'

'Decent quality, yeah? Sure they're not benzos?'

'. . . I'm sure.'

'You know where it came from?'

'Yes. Take one . . . now . . . if you like.'

'I don't take any o this shite,' I said.

'Didn't think so . . . chief.'

I tossed a pill out to her across the table. It landed next to the soggy mushroom roots. She picked up the knife again and carefully broke the pill into two halves.

'Jacob,' she said.

The boy came to her side – blank face, darker now.

'Eat . . . your mushroom, chief,' she said to me.

I stretched forward and took that knife of hers and cut the mushroom cap into two. 'You want us to just eat this raw?'

'That's the best way . . . This will prepare you for . . . burun . . . danga.'

'What the fuck is this burundanga?' I said.

I waited.

'Bollocks,' I said, 'This isn't worth me time.'

The little boy fed half an E inside her cracked lips and then swallowed the other half himself.

I was here now. I gave them Frank's money.

The Witch passed it to Jacob to count under the crucifix. He placed the lot in a petty-cash box hidden in one of the cupboards behind his head, next to another mushroom patch.

'Chief, are you old enough to remember . . . Wakes week?'

'"The Wakes! The Wakes! The jocund wakes!"' I

pocketed the gear with a chunk of my mushroom and got up to leave.

She said: 'How do you know that poem?'

'Dunno, Maggie,' I said. 'Me mam used to sing it.'

Jacob came over to show me out the room. I stopped when he snatched my wrist and held my hand palm up. His small fingers were damp and tough.

'Well?' I said.

'Don't let her go with him,' he said, dropping my hand without even looking at it.

'Go with who? Let who go?'

He pointed at the door. 'Her – out there.'

I looked back at the wheezing Witch one last time.

'Bane . . .' she grinned. '. . . Never come back to my house.'

The pimp made his way in as I came out. Jacob shut the door again.

I took the empty spot on the sofa next to the prozzy. A short blue dress clung to her well.

'What's your name, love?'

'Pearl,' she said with a smirk.

'What's your name, love?' I said again.

'. . . Gemma.'

'I'm Bane, Gemma.'

'Iya Bane.'

'Iya Gemma. I think I need a word.'

'Yer avin one now.'

I coughed into my fist. 'It's a job to in here. You fancy gettin some air?'

Her cute brow forked, interested. 'Now what d'yer wanna speak tuz about?'

'Well—'

'Am on the game.'

'I know that, love.'

She gave a smile, like she thought I was as loony as the rest of them. 'Then yer know yull need to speak to our Den when ee comes out o there.'

'I don't think he'll wanna speak to me.'

'If there's so much as a fiver left in yer wallet ee'll be all bloody ears.'

I took out a twenty.

'Best give it im. Ee'll only tek it off us if ee finds it.'

'Why would he find it?' I said.

Gemma laughed. Her teeth were good.

'You're sweet for this racket,' I said, watching my money disappear. 'What do y'know?'

'Ah know it can get fuckin scary. N Den avin a pretty paddy cos ee's mashed on a bit o crack is nowt.'

'There's nowt pretty about him.'

'Den? Ee's a softy most o the time. Trust us. Yer don't know im.'

'So what's been scarin you lately then?'

'Yer sure you're not lookin fer business?'

I asked again.

She drew her long legs up on the sofa, folded them underneath her, turned her body towards me. 'Girls . . .' she went. A dramatic pause to hook me. '. . . Dyin.'

Some student puff tried to pass me a badly rolled

joint. I waved it away and Gemma took it off him instead.

'Girls?' I said.

She nodded as she took a toke.

'Dyin?'

She coughed out a ball of smoke. 'Dyin.'

'Like who?'

She took another drag and then let it go. 'Yer read bout that girl what them bastards left dead on Stockport Road?'

I said I had.

'Honest to God, right, ah fuckin knew er. She were called Alice. Den took er in jus this week. She stayed wiv us n everythin.'

'How long had she been stayin with you n this Den?'

'Jus three nights, like. Never met er before that.'

'N where is this you're livin?'

'Know Cast Street? Up near—'

'Cast Street? Wythie?'

'Yeah. We was livin nearer town, up off fuckin Wellington Road but we moved back. Yeah, it's deffo not bout that postcode. Plenny o business but—'

'What about this Alice . . .' I said – but the room was starting to turn. Some of this could've been heading somewhere but my mind was getting lost on the way. I snatched the next spliff and dibbed it out on the arm of the couch. It turned some spilt candle wax black.

'Ayyyy . . .' said the white Rasta, complaining.

'Say summat else,' I said.

He looked away.

I turned to Gemma. 'Look, Alice Willows was a mate o mine.' I stood up and held out my hand. She looked at me carefully for a moment then took it.

Gemma slid her back down the wall – holding her hem, keeping her dress over her thighs as she sat on the cold floor.

I paced the deck a bit to clear my head. 'Love, you warm enough out here?'

'Fine, love.'

'Go on,' I said, 'about Alice.'

She huffed, tipping forward and her hair fell in her eyes. It was like she'd just thought of something funny. 'Thing is, right – that night, she were wearin me three undred squid Dee n Gee shoes. The night they did er, ah mean. Ah wunt be arsed but them weren't knock-offs. Ad pinched um but all the same.'

'So how did my Alice end up with your shoes?'

'Well ad let er av um fer Kitchen Club. She'd never bin before n she dint av owt decent enough. Den says ee'll fetch um from coroners.'

'Fetch what?' I said.

'Me shoes! But will ee fuck. Ee'll never. N like ad want um now. Bloody dead-girl shoes! That's mad, init? Don't yer think? Poor thing, she died wearin um. Me shoes! Probly gunna be buried in um n all.'

'Go back,' I said, crouching next to her. 'How'd you meet Alice?'

'Den as a few girls on the go. Ah know what yer thinkin but ee's not – ee's not wiv um. Ee's jus wiv me.

Anyway, sometimes they crash at ours fer a bit – two or three of um, right – but they move on after a while. Either they stop usin. They start usin. Ee knocks one about when they mouf off or do summat daft n they fuck off. She were one of um. Den can be sweet but ee can be a sod. Only I know ow to keep is ed screwed on. Six munf me n im av bin a team. Six munf. D'yer know ow long that is? N am not on smack. Six munf. If anythin ee's the bloody druggy in our ouse.' She paused and tilted her head back and wiped her hair off her face. Her eyes were gorgeous. 'Ah dint get a proper chance to know your Alice. She seemed alright, like. Nice enough. She wan't much of a looker, though. Slim n that, but she were jus Plain Jane, yer know? N ah mean – she wan't clean. But, yer know – none of us – she dint deserve—'

'Was she injectin?'

'She ad the marks but ah never seen er. She smoked it. She were on the rocks, by the bloody Transit load. Downers n all that, but Den can't always elp out wiv that stuff. Poor cow, she were a bit fried.'

I touched her arm and said: 'So what was Alice Willows doin – in *your* best shoes – down at the Kitchen Club that night?'

Gemma leaned in close with a clever smile. 'Workin, love – what yer think?'

The front door to the Fold opened and we both turned our heads. Gemma's pimp came towards us, chest out, mouthing off. Gemma stood up like lightning. 'Den, jus leave im! We're not fuckin doin owt!' She

37

flailed about in front of him to try and keep him away. He pulled her hair back and her head met the wall.

He started to yell something at me. I thumped him in the eye but he didn't go down, he just held his face – stood there in shock, hobbling around, swearing. I dragged Gemma away – those good legs quick marching as we came down the stairwell and outside.

'Gem! Gem! Get back ere!' We could hear him screaming himself hoarse from the top of the stairs. 'GEEEEEEMMMM! Al fuckin kill yer!'

It was dusk over the craters of shit in the courtyard when we came out. The sky was moving – purple, grey.

I walked us along fast. 'Stop it! Let go!' Gemma said, trying to yank her arm out of my fist. I carried on until she shrieked my name: 'Bane!'

I was surprised she'd remembered it. We were both breathing hard. She tried to pull away again but I squeezed her hand until she yelped. 'Wake up. If I let you go back, he batters you.'

She looked down at her shoes, when she looked back up her bottom lip was still on the floor. 'Av done it now. Av fuckin done it. This is it. Ee's gunna go mad at us. Shit! Shit!' I let go of her. She stomped her feet. She was teary, strange, shaking.

I said: 'You did nowt. He's scum, love. Y'know it.'

'Al-al jus av to let im calm down a bit, yeah? Ah jus ope ee . . . oh God . . .'

'Listen,' I said, 'you hungry?'

'What?'

'Do you wanna get summat to eat?'

'No, ta.'

I touched her shoulder gently. 'There's me car. Our lad Gordon's mindin it, you'll be right.'

' . . . Yeah. Sod it. Yeah, ah do.'

'Gemma, I'm sorry if I squished your hand, love. Are we good?'

'We're good.'

'How's the head?'

The miserable frown went. 'It's alright,' she said.

'He's just scum.'

'We off or what?'

I got her over to the car and Gordon rolled the front passenger window down. 'Yer took yer fuckin time,' he said. 'Oo's she?'

'Get in the back,' I said.

'Charmin. What's yer name?' he said to Gemma.

'Pearl,' she said, leaning through the window frame, all smiles.

'Gordon.' He was almost laughing.

'Let him get out,' I said, 'you can get in front.'

I got in the driver's side and she buckled herself in. We had to move our seats forward since Gordon took up most of the back bench.

'Oi, ow'd yer manage to cop off ere? They mad fer it in there or what?'

I twisted round to mouth him a pretty word.

Then Gemma squealed. 'Oh fuck!'

Something hit the front of the car.

I turned back and saw Gemma cowering under the

dash. I looked out the windscreen. Den flashed a blade. 'Get er out. Get er fuckin out. Al kill er!' Sweat was pumping out of his face. He was taking run-ups and kicking in my front panel.

'Gordon,' I said. 'Before we lose the fuckin bumper.'

Gordon climbed back out and introduced himself to Den. He took the knife off him without any mither – gave him a brick fist instead. His slaps were middle-weight quick and heavyweight hard. The crackhead was down after a one-two. Next the Rockport boot went in. It wasn't long before our Gordon was having a ball.

Gemma buried her face in my Harrington and cried.

'Gordon!' I yelled. 'Pack it in. Enough.'

When the three of us were all in the car again I turned the engine over and sounded the horn. Den rolled out from under the left wheel before I could run him over.

Out of Bonsall Street and away, I passed Gordon back a dashboard cloth and he wiped his bleeding knuckles.

5

TEA N CHIPS?

I GAVE GORDON the gear I'd bought from the Witch and dropped him off in town. He'd head back to Frank's to dish it out between the lads so they could shift it in the clubs that weekend. Not a word about the change of supplier, I'd said – just like that. If the batch came up as shit, Frank might be fucked off. Not that he'd mithered with testing it himself for a while. But Frank cared a lot. He thought he was one of the old guard. And if Frank gave them out to a few faces who mattered and we had a few fuckups on our plate, I'd own up and Frank would send us back with shotguns. Not that we had shotguns. Shit like that tended to just appear when we thought we needed it. Some bugger knows some other bugger. The grief would only start when we tried to make it all disappear again. Frank. He'd probably cut my bollocks off for going there in the first place.

Gemma was channel-hopping on the car radio. I took a hand off the steering wheel and found her Kiss 102. Our fingers met.

'You a fan o this one?' I said.

'Oo is it?' she said, turning it up.

'Fugees.'

Her head nodded. 'Yeah. S'alright, this. Ah like music, me.'

'They were on the telly the other night.'

'These were?'

'Yeah.'

'Doin this one?'

'Yeah.'

'We need a telly.'

'What happened? Last one packed up?'

'Ah fuckin boot packed it up one Saturday. Right through bloody screen!'

'Den?'

'. . . Yeah.'

'Must o been gutted his lottery numbers didn't come up.'

'Ee's a sod.'

'What make was it?'

'JVC. Dead dear, them.'

'Want another?'

'Ay?'

'I've got a mate.'

'Av yer?'

'Sorted. Give us a week.'

The shutters were down on most of the food places in the Northern Quarter. We parked up, and I took her inside an empty Greek café off Thomas Street.

I said: 'Can I grab a brew, love? Put a drop o milk in for us.'

Gemma said: 'Yeah, same fer us, love.'

A chubby madam with a brown lined face and black eyes started up an angry tea machine. Behind her there were blown-up photos of parcelled scran on little stacked trays. It could've been deep-fried tarantula. Not my menu. I don't even go for kebabs. She wiped her hands on her apron and said: 'Anything else?'

Gemma looked at me.

'I'm buyin,' I said.

'Chips, ta,' she said.

'Tea n chips?'

'Yeah.'

'Why not.'

I gave Madam a note and she handed me back a lot of change. She said she'd bring the teas over. We sat by the window and looked out at the neon signs across the street. Gemma said she could do with a fag. I told her I didn't smoke.

We could hear the fryers going.

The tears had upset her mascara – the fresh coat swollen and sooty in the bright lights of the caff.

'Where did we get to?' I said.

'Ay, love?' she said, eyes leaving the window. Her skin was pale but not pasty – her forehead a little shiny.

'Back outside the Fold,' I said. 'About Alice. Can you tell us why she was workin at the Kitchen Club that night, somewhere she'd never been before?'

'Den arranged it all. Ee'd got friendly wiv the management, or so ee said – started shiftin coke down there n that. Ee'd get asked to bring a few of us down fer them afterparties.'

'So Den takes Alice to the Kitchen Club. Why not you?'

'I ad uva commitments.'

'You had other what?'

She leaned in with her arms crossed. I felt her toe knock on my shin three times. 'I – was – on.'

The lady brought us our teas in chipped white mugs.

Neither of us took sugar.

Gemma locked her fingers round hers and gazed down at the heat rising off the top. She lifted it, took a sip, frowned, pouted over it and blew softly. I just sat there watching its surface wrinkle like it was something new, something from another planet.

She said to me: 'Yer right, love?'

I nodded. 'So he brings Alice to make a bit o cash. You lend her your best heels. Did he go down with anyone else? Any other birds?'

'Well ee got imself picked up from ours. There was already anuva girl in the back.'

'Who picked him up? Someone from the club?'

'Ah dunno. Yeah, probly. It were in a big dock-off car.'

'What type o car?'

'A black one,' she said. 'Fancy.'

'Helpful. Cheers.'

Gemma laughed. 'Well, ah don't bloody know, do ah? A Merc. Coulda bin a Merc. A big one.'

I wondered if it had been Terence Formby himself.

The chips followed the teas. Gemma poured on the sex and violence, grabbed a fork and stabbed at them in a dainty rush.

'Tell us about this other bird,' I said.

'God, yer love askin these questions, you do.' She harpooned more chips – two at a time, and stuffed them into her mouth. A combination of the munchies and growing up with older siblings, I thought. She pushed the plate of chips nearer me, swallowed what was in her gob and said: 'Want one, love?'

'I'm good. Go on.'

'Okay, Den n ah were rowin. Ad followed um out to the car to give im ard time bout some shit or uva. Yer Alice were keepin quiet, she were mashed. Ad elped er do er make-up n fair play to er, yeah – she were lookin as good as she got. Den got in the front o that fancy car n Alice got in the back. N there she were – this uva one – already sat there on uva side. She's a proper stunner from what ah saw – the bitch – well out of is bloody league, anyroad. Ad seen er the las time they'd picked im up. So it were twice ah seen her. Ah don't know er name or story or owt but ah do know yer wunt find er wiv er tits out wiv the rest, down on Store Street, shaggin in the back o some old bloke's banger.' Gemma stopped to spool another chip in her mouth. She chewed: 'N get this – she dunt even speak any English. Least that's what Den told us when ah asked after er once. That's all ee said of er. She dunt speak English. Cow's done grand then, ah said.'

I gave my tea a go. It was muck.

'What does she look like?' I said.

'Bagabones.'

'Like you?' I went, wondering just where she was putting it all.

Her toe found my shin again. 'Ay, you! No, ah mean proper dead skinny. Like them on catwalk. A bloody tree branch.'

'What else?'

'Dark air. A real looker.'

I said: 'You sure it wasn't that Egyptian girl – Safir? The rich one in the papers, they found her dead on the same night.'

'That model? That were awful n all. But nah, love – nah, it wan't er.'

'Where's she from – No English?'

'Fuck knows. Den might av said. Ah dunno. She's got this mark on the top of er arm, dead big – yer know like a tattoo, but it's not.'

'Birthmark?'

'Yeah, right ere – this one – it's shaped like a . . . like a crown.'

'A vanilla-cream crown?'

She started to shake her head and then laughed.

'Them your milk teeth?' I said.

'Ay?'

'You're a smiler.'

She hid her grin. 'That's what ee used to say.'

I gave my tea another go. It was still muck. Gemma tried hers again – she pulled a face as she drank it. 'Psshh . . . rank that. Can see bloody tea leaves.'

'Who killed Alice, Gemma?' I said.

She pushed her tea to the end of the table. 'Dunno. Den come back on is own that night – dead early. Ee brought some gear back wiv im – dunno what – coke, ah think. Ee said ee jus left um all to it. Ah think ee'd bin given summat to old fer somebody. Somebody ee wanted to get in bed wiv. Like fer dealin ah mean, not like some uva cow.'

'I know what you meant, love.'

'Next we eard – Alice were on the news. Den'll know more – ee always does but ee ant said.'

I stopped at an off-licence and got Gemma some fags, a pack of peppermint gum and a music weekly. She wouldn't let me talk her out of going home. She said Den wouldn't have gone back so soon and she'd have time to sort herself out while he calmed down. She said this happened a lot, just not usually as bad. I said with a bit of luck, our Gordon would have put him in A&E for the night. I drove her to Cast Street.

I parked halfway up the street, switched the radio

off but kept the engine running. She lived three doors down from our Jan.

'Are you sure he's not in there? D'you want us to come inside?'

Gemma laughed and went: 'Ah want yer not to worry, love. Al be right.'

'What the fuck are you doin this for, ay?'

'What d'yer think?' She laughed at me again.

She saw that I wasn't finding it funny.

She put her lips to mine.

'Gem, if the low life ever loses its appeal – give us a ring, yeah?'

'Ha-ha! N you, love. N even if it don't.' She grinned madly, got out and crossed the street. I watched her put her key in the front door, toss me a wave and disappear inside. The hall light came on, followed by another light upstairs.

I kept the radio off and drove back into town.

6

TERENCE FORMBY'S KITCHEN CLUB

TERENCE WAS A crook like Frank and for rivals, they had a pretty good working relationship – they even had Boxing Day dinner together one year. Wives and all. Terence was about ten years older than Frank but in much better shape. He was slim round the waist to say he liked a drink, had a foul mouth, a neat silver head of hair and a good chin. He was newly free of a third trophy wife and it would be a while before he'd settle on a fourth. Terence only ever came out in a flash Hugo Boss suit, polished Italian shoes flooring the pedals of his XK8 or Land Cruiser like he was cock o the walk.

Formby earned the most from two nightclub venues. He lived above the first, the Kitchen Club, with its choosy coke-sweating doormen who thumbed-up first-division footballers, page-three totty and no-names off the box. The second was a grubby strip club, north of the ring road. There may have been more, a massage parlour in Chinatown was rumoured to be his under somebody else's name, but that was all I knew of. He was Salford-born, so it goes. His old man had been a baker.

I nipped back to Frank's to get some decent grub, pinched a special that had been sent back to the kitchen and washed it down with a Kaliber. I didn't see Gordon but on the way out I saw Frank giving one of the foreign chefs a rough time of it – outside behind the cage by the bottle bins. Frank wiped his Brylcreem quiff back into shape. Said a few more nasty words. Frank and his illegals. The waiters got fists to the stomach when they cocked up, you don't want to leave a mark on them if they're serving out front. But chefs? They're in the back. No problems at all.

I didn't say hello.

I left the motor on St Mary's Parsonage and walked back to Deansgate. It was just after eleven.

The Kitchen Club.

A long queue of tall heels and short frocks. I clocked the meatheads on the door – I was pally with one of the bouncers but it must have been his Friday off. I lapped round the back and tried my luck on the blue iron door. Some naff house tune thumped from inside, louder when the peep window slid open: 'Fuck off.'

I said: 'It's one o Frank's boys. I'd like a friendly word with our good Terence.'

'Fuck off.'

'Fair enough, mate. I know where I'm not wanted. Goodbye cruel world.'

'Bane . . .'

'Jamie, lad? Didn't see you on the door.'

He opened up. I shook hands with the silverback in a Crombie.

'That gym needs to start chargin you rent,' I said.

'Lookin alright yerself, these days.'

'Cheers.' I said, still flexing my sore fingers.

'Bin goin this new one outta town, mate. But not bin this week. Not ad much chance wiv work n that. Fuckin pigs wantin statements from us all bout this dead bird meant two mornins down bloody station. Missin me beauty sleep, mate. It's bin all go down ere though, ah tell yer.'

'I bet.'

Jamie's eyeballs worked faster than his tongue. He needed steering off the charlie tonight. I followed his fridge-freezer of a back. He could have given our Gordon a run for his money.

This way in took you behind the bar and led upstairs to a staffroom and up again to Formby's posh flat. These were plush for back-of-club rooms.

Jamie took me over to a curvy bird in a plain green frock at the bottom of some carpeted stairs. She was thirty-fivish – had a hard face, a 300-watt tan-bed colour and a clipboard. She put the clipboard down and picked up a glass of something blue from a table. The subwoofers came through from the main room – hard enough to make her drink dance. She had a fancy haircut – upset by a daft microphone headpiece that looked more for show than anything.

'Is that thing switched on?' I said to her.

'Is it bugger,' Jamie said. 'But dunt she look fab? Shell, tek im up to see Terence if ee's decent . . . is ee decent?'

'Ah wan't plannin on checkin,' she said. She looked me over with a practised coldness and said: 'Ee's up there avin a bit of a private get-together. It's your funeral, chick.'

'You'd look good in black,' I said.

Her mouth twisted into a smile.

7
DIGGIN

I WALTZED IN solo. Formby had a swanky big pad and I followed the boom of his voice to an open living room. The music in the club downstairs couldn't be heard from up here. Not even a vibration.

'Bane, int it?'

'Spot on.'

'Shell jus told us yer were poppin up.'

'Yeah, that's right.'

He shook my hand and dropped it. 'Sit down, son. Get yourself a fuckin drink. I hear yer came in through the back?'

There was charlie and booze and a pack of cards spread on the glass coffee table. Plenty of cash. I sat down on a sofa seat, picked up a bottle of brandy by the neck and read the label. 'Didn't fancy the queues.'

'Don't fuckin blame yer. Should've rang us before. Someone would've got yer on the guest-list.'

'I'm here now.' I put the brandy back down.

'Ow's our Frank doin?' Terence said.

'Well. He's very well.'

'Good to hear, son. Bet ee dunt know ow to party like this though, does ee? That fat bugger can't even get in is bloody catsuit no more. Shake, rattle n sausage roll.'

We all made sure we laughed.

The *we*: a coked-up TV weatherman, two councilmen and a first-division midfielder plus his tagalongs. There were some other fruity lounge lizards and local crooks mooching here and there — small-time, still saving up for the Cheshire home and second-hand bimmer.

There were also a good five or six clearly trafficked Eastern-European birds willowing about the place in shaky stilettos, a couple with their bony arses on some tub of lard's pinstriped knee, each one doped to the nines. Gloomy things. They looked like broken dolls.

This was all pretty new to me. But the stories were getting old.

And then there was this one sat to my right.

This one was glamorously thin. All lips and eyes and cliff-edge cheekbones — body lost somewhere inside a flimsy minidress. Hair was dark blonde, cut just above shoulder-length and moussed back off her face. Her earrings were Cyndi Lauper dangly shells and crosses — a Eurotrash giveaway.

I stretched an arm out on the sofa back and brushed

her shoulder. Her face made its way round to mine in no hurry, huge slate eyes working a steady blinking pattern. I didn't fancy my chances in a staring contest.

'That a scar, a tat or a birthmark?' My hand moved down to the top of her arm. I traced around the plum crown shape on her skin with an index finger.

'Don't bother, lad,' Terence went, refilling his drink. 'She dunt know a fuckin word o Queen's English. Not a fuckin word.'

'Did Den bring her round?' I said.

Terence sat back with a full glass. 'Oo?' He tightened his face.

'That slimy sod mithers Frank every other week.'

He gave me the benefit of the doubt. 'There were a time when that Den might bring a bird or two down to the club. Filthy slags, dear me. But ow could ee compete wiv this?' He held his arms out like he was offering me it all.

'N where does all this new crumpet live?'

'Why? Yer thinkin bout tekin one ome to meet yer mam?'

I slapped my heart. 'My poor mam's gone, Terence.'

'Shame, cos ad recommend it. They won't show yer up, don't even answer back.'

The midfielder roared with phony laughter.

Terence leaned forward again. 'Yer couldn't afford these, son. So enjoy um now while yer can. Cos ad be careful.'

'How d'you mean?'

'Yer not read the news? Dead Safir n that missin wog

that lived on er shoulder? Made the nationals this mornin.'

'Saw a bit in the locals yesterday.'

'That fairy Abdul doin a runner. Fuckin daft Paki.'

'Knew her well did you? *Safir*.'

'She liked it down ere. We give er a table.'

'N who's got it now?'

He didn't say anything to that.

I spotted a surveillance camera in the top far corner of the room. 'Beefin up security nowadays?'

Formby tried to smile: 'Pigs've bin at the CCTV to see oo she left wiv. But our new security system ant bin workin proper. We jus got it up n runnin yesterday. Smile, lad. Candid camera.' He turned and pointed. I looked straight at it. 'Give us a wave, Bane,' he said.

A bit much. The flat, as well as the club. I turned away. What was she like then, ay? Worth a go?'

'I tek it yer don't know then?'

'I take it I don't,' I said – like I was hanging off his every fucking word.

Formby's face screwed up as he gave his next words a dress rehearsal in his head first. 'Obnoxious little cow. Jus soddin perfect. Yud wanna cut er jus to knock the smile off er face. Yer know that type? Yeah – yer do don't yer? Course ee does. She were young n loaded n a right looker. But open that one up n we're talkin rotten to the core.'

'Somebody did.'

'Ay?'

'Open that one up.'

'Fuckin aye.'

'What was her poison?'

He took a big swig and knocked the lot back. Refilled.

'Shaggin, Bane. She loved shaggin. Not jus coke. Not whizz. Not jus spendin er daddy's cash. Shaggin. Safir the fuckin sex monster. Jus wait till them tabloids get wind.'

At the rate Terence was blabbing, that wouldn't be too far off. God bless the charlie.

So I tried my luck: 'She was bein blackmailed then?'

He pulled a passing bird down into his lap. 'Steady. Yuv only bin ere ten minutes n you're already life o the party. What's wiv all this diggin, lad?'

'I'm not diggin.'

'You are!' he said, slapping the girl's grey thigh for emphasis, drink swinging in his other hand. 'I'm nursin a bloody semi ere n you're makin us chat bout this bollocks. Did Frank wanna know the goss? What the fuck are we doin?' He raised his glass. 'Let's fuckin av it!'

The lads cheered. The dolls didn't get a vote.

I looked into the face of the skinny bird with the birthmark next to me – not a blink from her. Not a thing.

Terence settled down and said to me with a shark grin: 'Now stay, av a drink, av a laugh or fuck off.'

About an hour later and Terence was already a goner. He was rolling around on his Egyptian carpets, crying with laughter, knocking over his own vases and imported brandy bottles. Most of the broken dolls had lost their clothes.

I was sat down on the floor in a corner with my back to the wall, Harrington off, a dead drink in my hand, just watching the freak show. Next to me was this young lad, twenty-odd, a queer, who said his name was Neil. He was a rum addition to the Kitchen clique. Or maybe not. Neil told me I'd suit mascara. After I'd swapped a magic mushroom for more make-up tips, he told me that he'd seen Alice here, Tuesday night.

He said: 'Ah reckon yer mate Den got asked to bring someone down fer Safir n er lot. Ah saw er. She were a right tarty madam, yer know? No offence lovey, but – ah mean – she wan't much to look at. N well, no one shagged er ere – only Safir, right – ah reckon she took a shine to er – asked er to come wiv um once they moved on. I wan't invited. String along the extra puffter, why don't yer?'

'Sorry they didn't string you up like my Alice?'

'Ah were only tekin piss – am sorry, lovey. Yer care a lot, don't yer?'

'Was Safir a lez?' I said.

'Lovey, Safir were all sorts.' He took an eyeliner pencil out of a trouser pocket, perched up on his knees and grabbed hold of my wrist. He began scribbling a phone number up the inside of my forearm.

'Now, look, mate, I'm not into owt—'

He said: 'Ate to disappoint but this int me number, lovey. Now this – this belongs to someone oo am pretty sure yud like to av a brew wiv. Ee were ere that night wiv us but this one left wiv Safir, yer sweet art, the whole pissin lot of um.'

'So what happened?'

'God knows. Whatever fuckin appened – spooked im bloody no end. So ring im. Ask fer our Gerry.'

'Gerry?' I said. 'What does this Gerry look like, then?'

Neil pouted. 'Bout so igh, spiky blond air, not much meat on im.' I moved my arm as he finished off the last digit. 'Be careful or yull smudge it. Our Gerry's alright, scrubs up a treat weekend after dole money's in. Gone straight t'pot by Monday.'

'This your boyfriend?' I said.

He popped the eyeliner in his gob and pinched my cheek. 'Now n then. Don't be jealous.'

A random shout made us both look. Formby's party was in full swing. Only her – the quiet one, Birthmark, No English, the bloody Doll Princess – still had most of her kit on.

'Oi Neil,' I said, pointing to her with my drink hand, 'Did *she* leave with um that night?'

'Er? Lady Muck? Oh aye. But not gunna get much out of er are yer? Now, if one knew er mother tongue.' Laughter. 'Whatever that may be. Fuck knows.'

She wasn't doped up like the rest of them. She was putting it on. I knew it. 'What's her name?' I said. 'What's the story?'

Neil covered his mouth, giggled. His shoulders shrugged.

'Is this just smack this lot are on, or what?' I said.

'Yer mean – our lady company?'

'Yeah.'

'Dunno what it is, lovey, but it sure zaps fire out, dunt it? But then again, it's not summat I av to deal wiv.'

'You've been a right help, Neil. Nice one.'

He giggled again. 'Ah do me bloody best. Anyway . . .' He pointed at the phone number on my arm before he got up and strutted across the room. He was necking the midfielder before long. Nobody made a fuss. Nobody even noticed. That camera watched us all.

I left my dead drink and went for a wander.

8

THE CAMERA'S EYE

I TOOK THE tour of Formby's flat alone. His bedroom was still empty. It was more modest than I was expecting, mostly taken up by a big double bed. The room had a low ceiling, a rusty-red paint scheme and some dark wood furniture. There was a large window that looked out onto the back. I opened a door and found an en-suite bathroom, closed it again, went back and shut the bedroom door. There were two small monitors on Formby's cabinet table on the far side of the room. Each screen was split into four squares. On the top left – the view behind the tills down in the club. I could make out the punters, dance floor heaving like a sea of cockroaches. Top right showed the bouncers giving a pisshead a hard time by the main entrance. The back entrance was quiet enough and we had Formby's trashed living room framed nicely in the last square. I could see Formby out cold on one of the sofas, his party still lively around him – the dolls taking it like troopers.

There were faxes on his desk, bits of stationery and a gram of coke. I forced a letter opener into the lock of his bureau. He had a stash of knock-off designer sunglasses, but it was the top drawer that had the goods. I took out a brown envelope addressed to him, opened it up and pulled out the first black-and-white photograph.

It showed me two sweethearts sucking face on a bedspread, both in their birthday suits – a touch blurred – taken through a window with a zoom lens.

Two birds. A skinny white European with a birthmark on her arm and a dark Egyptian model – a student, a socialite, an heiress. There were plenty of snaps in the envelope – a bloke in some of them, tattoos up his back, making himself useful. There wasn't a decent one of his face. It was as if he knew the game. Or maybe he'd done the editing himself. I sifted through the lot.

No Alice.

Both girls got a mouthful of cock. Safir was the real goer, putting her teammates to shame – an arc of jet black hair was plastered over her face in two shots – full lips set wide in a massive grin. But things really began from the neck down. I came back to the first print and turned it over. Spidery male handwriting:

Terence –
Video still set for Tuesday.
– Lance.

I heard the bedroom doorhandle turn behind me.

'Iya, love,' I said.

She shut it again and came into the room.

'Somebody's not bloody camera-shy,' I said, waving a mucky photo at her. 'Now that's your best side.' I showed her another one, and another. 'Formby should keep this lot in the safe. These locks aren't worth a chocolate key.'

She ignored me, walked into the en-suite bathroom – turned on the light.

'What's your name?' I shouted through. I waited a few seconds before asking again.

Nothing.

'Mine's Bane. Henry Bane.'

Nothing.

The party in there grew louder. The monitor screens showed me Formby coming to on the sofa. I snatched up the gram from his desk and followed her into the bathroom and locked us in. She was staring at herself in the wide wall-mirror. I spun her round so she was facing me and shook her by the throat. A stiff lock of hair jumped out of place and landed over her eye. She looked at me – empty, unimpressed.

I wiped her hair back in place and then pushed some of Formby's coke up her nose, crushing the other nostril for her. She did it. Twice. It didn't wake her up. She was just a no-goer. I could hear my blood ticking behind my ear, feel my forehead sweating. I kissed her. She didn't kiss me back. I'd rubbed her lipstick onto her cheek. I was angry, embarrassed.

'Who snuffed Alice n Safir?' I said, lifting her up onto the marble surfaces. 'You fuckin know, don't you? Just tell us who did it.' I held her against the mirror. 'Was it Formby? This Lance?'

We faced off like this for a while, up close, breathing in and out, getting ourselves nowhere. Her eyes fixed on mine – she took a blind grab at my hard-on. Sharp little teeth started chewing my lip – a dry tongue went down my throat.

Someone elsewhere in Formby's flat screamed.

We both turned our heads to the sound. It was a girly scream, followed by some words. Some begging. It was definitely Neil. Then some other blokes' voices took over.

'Don't go runnin off,' I said.

I shut her in the bathroom and then opened the bedroom door a split.

There were lots of them.

I couldn't see enough from this angle to count how many. Terence Formby was slurring his words, swaying, down on his knees in the living room: 'Scuze me, son, but is that a fuckin submachine gun?' I heard him go, looking up at them all. He laughed and laughed and laughed.

I shut the door again and went over to the CCTV screens. I'd left the mucky photos spread across the tops of each monitor.

I counted four in the living room and clocked another two on the second camera, still marching up the back way over Shell's twisted body on the stairs.

I tipped to the window and saw a black Transit parked up out back. There was a lot of yelling in the flat now. These were bad lads. Balaclavas and heavy shooters. Not cheap burners. Stock-fitted submachine guns with foot-long silencers. They were working through the flat. I could hear the rattle and trod.

I thought about Maggie and her mushrooms. *Wakes Week*. Wakes. I thought I might die here tonight.

On the monitor: all the blokes had been herded into the middle of the front room. Terence took a burst in the chest first from one of the gunmen. I watched the clubbers dance downstairs oblivious. Formby's body dropped straight down. The lads let rip. The muted gunfire popped from the next room. I saw the first moments of the bloodbath crackle on the screens and then I came back into the bathroom and locked the door.

She was still sat on the surfaces, frock dragged up to her knickers. She stared at me, unblinking. Proud. Poised. Bloody superior.

I gripped her twig arm and she wiped my hand away like an insect.

'Who?' I said. 'Who the fuck are they?'

We heard the bedroom door being booted open.

Foreign words were barked from a metre away.

There was no way out.

She stretched slowly, arched her back and rubbed at her throat, then slid off the worktop, unlocked the bathroom door and opened it a couple of inches. She stood in front of the gap.

Somebody out there asked her something.

'Just me,' she said, walking out into the bedroom, closing the door on me.

I could hear something falling, splashing – a liquid – plenty of it, and then more shouting. Maybe five minutes passed. They were torching the place. Eventually, the voices went and I was left alone with just the smell for company. I coughed.

It was getting warm.

I opened the door and found the bedroom already on fire.

I could just about see the monitors – one still working, the girls being marched down the backstairs by the gang, the fucking Doll Princess in line with them. The last balaclava bloke was trailing the dregs of a fuel can behind him. He dumped it by the bottom stair, next to poor Shell and then left the camera's eye.

The photos were still lying on top of the screens. I couldn't reach them without getting roasted. I breathed through my shirt, leaned out into the corridor – just smoke and gore. Main room: blood on the walls bubbling in the flames, the heat was unreal, these fellers were cooking. I spewed and went back in, made it to the rear window.

I booted the glass through and elbowed out the rest of it, coughing up my lungs with the blast of clean air. I was blind. Smoke stole my exit and I crawled out and fell on the fire escape platform. My fingers went through the mesh. I stayed on my knees – bent double – choking up smoke and vomit.

When my ears started working, I could hear the crowds out front, street fights, howling traffic, the lick of sirens.

Farewell Kitchen Club.

I'd left my Harrington in Terence Formby's living room.

Gutted.

9

THE TORCH

I PUT THE overhead light on, took a biro and an old
petrol receipt out the glovebox and scribbled down the
number Neil had written on my arm. It was a job to
make out the ghost of each digit.

I saw my face in the rear-view streaked with sick
and soot and tried to give it a wipe with the bottom of
my shirt. I had a root about for something cleaner but
could only find the dashboard cloth crusty with Gordon's
blood. Looking better, but not my Sunday best, I started
up the car.

Deansgate was madness. The smoke from the Kitchen
Club was snaking around the taller buildings, choking out
the lights, hiding the bomb ruins down in Corporation
Street, climbing higher and higher. Flames had already
begun to spread across the row. The Fire Brigade were
trying to block the top end of Deansgate off and the foreign

cabbies weren't having any of it. I bullied my way further up the road. Outside another club, I spotted Gordon with a couple of our lads, everyone gawping at thc scene.

I stuck my head out the window and held down the horn. Things were getting so rowdy nobody even looked. 'Gordon! Oi! Get in!'

'Flamin fuckin Nora! Ay? Look at state o yer!' Gordon said, a great fat grin across his chops. He was trying to tune in a local news station while we queued up bumper-to-bumper just to sod off. 'Ha-ha! Mate, dint appen to see any o that back there did yer?'

'Leave it,' I said, knocking his hand from the radio to have a play. 'Shit.' I clipped a black cab trying to cut across the gridlock. That was it. I shot my revs up and upset the tyres. The cabbie wagged his fist, now in my rear-view as I drove away.

Gordon started: 'What yer reckon, mate? Anuva Paddy bomb? That Johnny reckons it were anuva Paddy bomb.' He was pulling his seatbelt round him as I raced up the gears.

I said: 'It wasn't the fuckin IRA n it wasn't a fuckin bomb. I told him. Once he'd heard it all the bugger was sorry he'd missed the fun.

'So where we off now?' he said. 'Don't we wanna check back in wiv the King? Ee's gunna love yer after this, mate.'

'Frank can fuck off. I need to check somethin else first.'

* * *

Back on Cast Street. Three trips in two days.

'Oh-aye, so yer took er back ome then did yer? After ad teken care o the fella fer yer. Jammy bastard.' Our Gordon shook his head, a big hand on my shoulder – pawing it like a jolly grizzly bear.

I said: 'Leave it out, lad. I took her back home, yeah. N that was that.'

'Bollocks. No time fer a pitstop?'

'Behave.'

We walked up to Gemma's house ignoring the kids in bovver boots and hoods pissing about with the BT box.

'Your pal's name is Den,' I said to Gordon. 'Might be in now. He's got answers to a few questions o mine. Hopefully, he might take a bit o convincin before he gives um.'

'Crack eds,' he spat.

I knocked on Gemma's front door and had a peep through the letter box.

'Lights on up there,' Gordon said.

'Let's have a gander round back,' I said.

The back gate was unlatched. So was the back door. Bad sign. Terrible sign.

I called out her name. 'Gemma!'

'I thought she were called bloody Pearl?' Gordon said as I went in first.

There was music playing. 'Song to the Siren' – The Chemical Brothers.

The bulb had gone in the hall but the landing light was on – so was the kitchen's. I nodded for Gordon to try upstairs and I followed the music to a radio on top of the kitchen fridge. The fridge door was open wide, wedged against the nose of an ironing board. Alphabet magnets on the door read:

WHO FUCIN STOL MY LPPY GIV 1T BK GEM X

Gemma was down to her underwear. She'd been ironing a cotton dress to wear when it happened. She just lay awkwardly against the sink cupboard in a mess of blood – those long legs looking daft splayed out in sharp crooked angles on the lino. Twelve rounds per second had taken the bottom half of her face away. I snapped the radio off. I could hear the blood dripping off the bottom of the fridge. The iron had burnt itself out. Dress still waiting to be pressed. I had to swallow to keep down whatever was left.

The glass had been knocked out of a mirror on the wall. I heard our Gordon crunching bits into his Rockport soles as he moved about upstairs.

The couch cushions were slashed in the front room, carpet ripped up, drawers and cabinets emptied. No telly. Just a space for a new one over in the corner.

Up the stairs – we found most of Den on the square landing. He had a makeshift sling around one arm, fresh from his run-in with Gordon just six hours ago. They'd really made sure he was dead.

Gordon spat over the banister, his face screwed up

in disgust. 'Bit much init?' he said. We stood there over the body, toes just shy of the soak patch on the carpet – the second shock of colour in this grim two-up-two-down. The impact from bullet holes in the wall had frosted the blood with plaster powder.

'Look up,' I said.

Gordon followed my eyes to the ceiling. 'Am lookin.'

'What's that?' I said.

'Fuckin loft, init? What does it look like?'

'Give us a hand.'

Gordon gave me a leg-up to reach the closed square hatch and I forced it open and poked my head through. There was a big hand torch just waiting up there within arm's reach.

I pulled myself through the hatch and picked it up.

'Batteries any good?' Gordon shouted.

'Bobbins.'

'Is it full o fuckin rats up there?' he said.

'No.'

With the weak torch on, I trod carefully along the boards. There was a gap in the brickwork that separated this terrace from the next. I shone the torch through it. I could just about see a smaller hole leading to the next loft after that.

I climbed through and carried on until I found what I was after. Den had nested his sweet stash on a St George's flag beach towel covering a strip of loft insulation above our Jan's bedroom. There was a couple of grands' worth of notes in the far corner, collecting dust. And on the towel I found two brown paper-wrapped bricks of something or other. I picked one up – it was a bit heavy for coke – but I could never tell. It was all much more than I was expecting from a little pond fish like Den. Then again, he liked to make friends.

I trapped the torch under my arm and carried the lot back with me.

'Owt wurf robbin?'

'Just this,' I said, hands full. 'Take the torch.'

'We best do one, mate.'

I said: 'I think you're right. N you'll have to get rid o those shoes.'

Footprints in the blood and glass.

10

IN THE NAME
OF SCIENCE

THE ALARM RADIO went off.

. . . it is thought the fire originally began in the
flat above before quickly spreading down to the
crowded nightclub . . . has left an unconfirmed
number dead and over a dozen injured in the
crowded evacuation. Manchester authorities still
suspect arson . . . terrorism has not been ruled out
. . . no organisation has come forward . . . current
health and safety regulations have been brought
into question by ministers in a statement over the
tragedy this morning . . . more details as they
develop . . . weather across Greater Manchester
continues to be bright and sunny with temperatures
even reaching . . . that was your 'News on the
Hour' with . . .

I rolled over – switched it off blind, knocking the fucking wire aerial into a cold brew. My everything was sore. I opened my eyes.

My gaff. My bed. 11.03 a.m. Light was breaking and entering through a rip in the curtains and I could hear the subs from next door's new multi-stack coming through the wall. I had to stop doing favours.

I sat up and had a think. So they'd called on Den on their way to the Kitchen Club and warmed up. Gemma had paid the pearly price for being in. Poor fucking cow.

Alice.

Gemma.

And I was still looking for that reason, that big bastard *why*. If they'd been searching for something that Den had stashed, they hadn't found it because now I had it. I wondered just how long it would be before the pigs realised that Formby and his lot didn't exactly go in the fire.

I got out of bed, got in the shower – still wondering. Half-dressed, I opened the front-room curtains and had a look out. It was going to be a fucking scorcher.

I'd split the two grand with our Gordon last night and dropped him off home. He'd keep his trap shut. Plus, I'd sorted him an extra wad so he could call in Frank's this morning with it and tell him I was grafting hard. It might have kept him off my back another day. It hadn't. Frank had left me two love poems on the answer phone.

Heart:

> Enry fuckin Bane. Now av not seen your sorry arse since Thursday. Where were yer las night? You're spose to be in this mornin, specially now wiv this Paddy shit goin on. Av got the Polacks cleanin the smoke n muck off the bastard windows. Now there's a job fer yer if yer show your mug before dinnertime. Johnny's busy. Av already put pies on Gordon's plate so ah need yer to— BEEP.

And soul:

> Fuck! N Bane, yer still got them keys fer the flat in Ancoats? Bring them in wiv yer. Ah don't wanna fuckin ear thev gone walkies. Ta-ra. BEEP.

The King and his whinge would have to wait. I called the number that Neil had given me last night before he'd been introduced to a submachine gun. I let it ring. Our mysterious Gerry didn't pick up. Nobody did.

In my kitchen, I opened a cupboard and took out Den's two bricks of gear from behind my branflakes. Coke? Smack? I still hadn't looked. I tore back a corner and couldn't tell. Maybe I was barking up the wrong tree. Or maybe it was something special. Something worth all this grief.

Forty minutes later and I'd trekked to Stretford, parked up as close as I could get, and was reaching under the passenger seat for my gifts.

I'd stuffed Den's dead torch, a pair of desert boots (size ten), Rockports (size fourteen), into a black bin liner and dumped them in the River Medlock on the way.

I came round the back and knocked on the door like I was the boys in blue. I could hear Stark rattling the chains and locks. He took his time about it.

'Bane?' Stark opened the door a gap.

'That's the one.'

'It's Saturday.'

'It is.'

'What, mate – what yer after?' He opened it the rest of the way – scraped a hand up his cheek stubble and rubbed his eyes.

'Is he up?' I said.

'No.'

'It's bloody dinnertime.' I invited myself in.

Through to the front room, up the stairs to the landing – Stark's bedroom door was already open so I tried the door on the right.

I snapped the big light on. The curtains were duct-taped shut. 'Rise n shine, mate. You're not fuckin Dracula.'

The Chemist was in bed, flat on his back – feet sticking out the bottom of the duvet. His top half shot up like in a cartoon. 'Stark! Stark!' he called out.

A third foot poked out from under the duvet. Small and white. Painted toenails in need of a touch-up. He had a bird in there with him. I was quite impressed, but she wasn't: 'The fuuuck!?' She groaned – her face in pillow. 'Shad up!'

'Stark!' he sat there in bed still yelling, like a kiddie fresh out of their favourite killer clown nightmare.

Stark came and stood next to me in the doorway. 'It's only Bane,' he said.

The Chem – this bearded stick insect on a come-down, reached for a pair of specs on his bedside table.

I said: 'Didn't know you usually wore contacts, lad?'

He held the glasses on his face and squinted at me. 'Christ, I thought yer were a bloody villain, Bane. Come to murder us fer me bountiful riches. What the fuck are yer doin ere?'

'Who's the bird?' I said.

He turned and looked her over while she dozed – still face-down, just ash-blonde hair. 'Jus a mate,' he said. 'She's up from Lundon fer weekend.'

'Lundon?' I whistled. 'You've been a dirty stop-out.'

She tried rolling herself over but couldn't fight gravity. She dropped an arm out of the duvet and it waved – a limp hello – then fell back under cover.

'What yer after?' the Chem said.

'To the lab, son. I've got you a present.'

He pulled on some clothes, and Stark and I followed him across to that room with the paint-stripped door. Little Friend from London stayed put.

Once we were inside, I showed him what I had. He unwrapped the first brick, bouncing the weight in his palm. 'This is a generous ki. It's not coke,' he said.

'No?'

'Stark,' he went. 'Fetch us both a brew.'

I nodded. Stark did as he was told.

The Chemist crumbled a corner off with his thumb, examined a brownish swirl in the off-white guck. He rubbed the pads of his forefinger and thumb together and made it into a powder. 'It almost looks erbal. But it's bin cut n re-rocked. I can tell yer that. But this could be anythin.' I watched him powder some more off onto a clean mirror slate on the worktop. He gathered up some short bottles of reagents and pulled out some hard-back books with broken spines that he'd stacked under-neath his portable telly. Shulgrin got a flick-through.

I watched him skim read for a minute. 'How long before you can tell us what's what?' I said.

He stopped flicking through the pages and looked up. 'Well, we can use the slow cooker or we can use the microwave.'

'Ay?'

He dropped a book down on the side next to the opened brick and walked past me to the doorway. He leant against the frame and said: 'Tara!' Then turned back: 'Bane, yer might've pulled a blinder ere, mate.'

There was a pause, then a voice: 'Downstairs! You've got a piss-poor selection of cereals. Frosties? Oh – my – days!'

The Chem looked back at me.

'N you,' I said. 'Thought you were a fairy.'

'Fuck off,' he said to me and then shouted down: 'Thought yer were in bed, love?!'

'You little boys woke me up, remember!?'

The Chem twisted round and said: 'Yer saw er. She were conked out a minute ago. Now she's givin lip.'

He called down the stairs: 'Tara, I'll tek yer out fer a butty. There's a caff jus round corner. Come up ere will yer. N tell Stark to urry up wiv them brews.'

'What caff?' I said.

He came back into the room. 'In the name of science.'

'Are you off your fuckin rocker?'

Tara and Stark came up after a minute. She was barefoot, lost somewhere inside a bloke's dressing gown – the sleeves had swallowed her hands. Her hair was washed-out, scribble.

Stark passed me a brew.

'Cheers. Not havin one?' I said to Tara.

'I'm a juice girl,' she said, crinkling her nose. She talked in that southern squeak.

'Bad luck. Better than coffee, I guess.'

'What's wrong with coffee?' she said.

'Muck.'

'T'isn't,' she said – all hurt. 'He's just got none in.'

'It's your life, love. Drink what you want.'

'I fucking will.'

'Muck,' I said, dying to smile.

She stared me out – still drowsy – tight lips a thoughtful line. When they unzipped she laughed. 'He's a right one, he is!' she said.

'This is Bane,' the Chem said.

'Bane, yeah? I'm Tara.'

I think we tried to shake hands.

'What's that?' she said looking at the mystery gear on the side.

The Chemist itched his beard. 'Interested in findin

out, sweet art?' Suddenly he'd become the gypo round Civic selling sunglasses in November.

Tara turned to me again. 'Is it any good?'

The Chem answered: 'Be the judge, love – n I'll pay fer yer train ticket ome. Sorry, when did yer say yer were fuckin off?'

'Cheeky, bastard. Glad to know you've enjoyed the company so much.'

'That I av – honest I av.'

'You'd been a marvellous host up till now.'

'N yuv bin a marvellous leech – I mean guest.'

That got a giggle out of the lads.

'You're a lanky ginger bastard, Trevor. Stingy with the weed and a sub-par shag.'

'"Trevor?"' Stark and I said it together, followed by a duet of '"Sub-par?"' when the second penny dropped.

'Piss off,' he said, giving us the V. He looked back at Tara. We all did. It was like she was a creature we'd queued up and paid to see – we were getting arsey waiting for it to do a trick.

She kept still. Her eyes bounced between the three of us. 'Boys, it's fucking ten in the morning.'

'It's quarter to one in the afternoon,' Trevor said.

Her nose crinkled again. 'I suppose it's better calorie-wise than breakfast. Best be a buzz.' She winked. 'Shall I put some in Bane's tea and have it that way?'

He said: 'Jus snort it, love – be way quicker. Not too much, jus a likkle line. Sides, no point ruinin a good brew, Stark makes a grand cupper.'

I raised my mug.

Tara locked on me again for a moment and said: 'You don't know what the fuck this is, do you?'

We all stayed quiet.

'Fuck it.'

'We know it's kosher,' Trevor said, 'So don't mither yerself bout that, jus sit down.'

Trevor pulled out a worktop stool, brushed the seat with his cuff and patted it. She sat down and pulled the big dressing gown tighter round her chest while he went and fixed her a line.

'Come on then!' she went.

I said: 'Hold tight, love – this one might tip you over.'

She snorted it straight off his front-door key. No time for banknotes.

'Well?' she said.

'Again,' Trevor said, poking the key back under her bugle.

'Hang on,' I said.

She blocked the other nostril, gave it another sniff – looking straight up at him as she did it, without blinking.

'That'll do,' I said.

'Any joy?' he said.

'First-class carriage alright? Wouldn't want someone like me mixing with the riff-raff.' She rolled her sleeve up and wiggled her nose about between her thumb and knuckle like she was shaking out those crinkles. Her cherry fingernails weren't wearing well, either.

'So Trevor, what next?' I said.

'Look, you lot fuckin christened us the Chemist. So

don't go actin like yud assumed it was on me birth certificate.'

'You were the Chem when I met you,' I said.

'Me n all,' Stark said as he went over to the stereo, ejected a cassette, flipped it over and pushed play.

A 2Pac tune was fading out – the DJ gabbing over the end, followed by a second or two of reception fuzz.

'Volume, mate,' Trevor said.

Nas's verse in 'Eye for a Eye' kicked in, mid-bar.

Stark spent hours taping pirate radio.

I heard Tara go: '. . . shit . . . giving me . . . fucking headache . . .'

'You got owt but rap?' I said. 'This one's not a big fan.'

'Don't be daft.'

'. . . turn it down,' she said.

'Turn it down,' I said.

Stark did.

Trevor smiled. 'Tara, she dunt do Mobb Deep. Dunt even go fer Biggie like any decent n discernin music appreciator. Ouse. Ouse. Ouse. Jus mindless bollocks. But rap – is – crap, right, love?'

We all looked down.

'Tara?' I said. 'You right, love?'

'Tara?' Trevor joined in.

Stark switched the tunes off.

'Tara?'

We were talking to a shop mannequin. Another broken doll.

'Bollocks. What yer give er? She's avin us on int she? That quick? She is – She is.' Stark rowed with himself.

She was sat there, still breathing, slowly, but nobody was home.

Trevor pulled her dressing gown open and checked her neck pulse. He felt her heart.

'I've an idea,' he said. He snatched his glasses off – gave them a rub on his shirt before putting them back on. 'Yer got a light?'

'Don't smoke,' I said.

'Course you don't. Stark?'

Stark fished into his joggers and passed him his lighter.

Trevor ducked, opened up a cabinet and rattled around for a moment. He popped back up, checking the valve on a rusty butane torch. 'Spark's broke,' he said. 'Come in andy these do, fer allsorts.'

I said: 'I bet.'

Tara looked on. Her face was mortuary-fixed. Trevor fired up the torch. The blue flame came to life – roared, settled. He balanced it, canister down on the worktop, aimed the bolt of heat towards Tara then asked her slowly and clearly if she could hear him. He tapped her hand and asked her again. She said she could, but not in a southern squeak. He told her to reach out and put her hand in the flame. Stark was stood on the opposite side of Tara to me, Trevor in front of her. Stark caught my eye and shot me a painful look like he had something important on his mind. A suggestion. An objection. Sometimes it can be hard to read the obvious.

I stopped Tara's hand at the wrist before she reached the torch flame. Nobody moved.

'Shit! She would've, she fuckin would've,' Stark said, his voice higher than usual.

'Fascinatin,' Trevor said.

'You're tapped.' I put her hand back on her lap.

I turned the flame off.

'Where's my cigarette . . . ?' Tara said slowly, her tongue in neutral.

Trevor squeezed a pipette full of reagent on the coke mirror he'd scraped a sample onto earlier. 'I reckon it could be packin some scopolamine derivative. Then there's plenny o deliberate impurities fer a bigger kick. I dunno. Extreme stuff this, mate. I read somewhere CIA use this sort o gear in South America fer like the ultimate truth serum.'

I said: 'What are you, the fuckin urban myth dispenser?'

'Don't av a go. It's true, mate.' He bent over Tara and examined her like a bull rhino playing doctor. 'This is encouragin.' He squeezed her bone-white cheeks together, pushing her thin lips into a pout and then rocked her head this way and that. Her eyes were like frosted glass.

'She's had enough,' I said. 'Get her a drink o water.'

'She can andle it, this one. Yer shoulda seen the shit she was pinchin off us las ni—'

'Now,' I said.

Trevor went: 'Stark. Go on, fetch er one. Use the sink downstairs.'

I asked what the side effects were.

'See fer yerself, mate. Our user, victim, Lundon lab munkey, shall retain consciousness though is open to what yer might call extreme suggestion, interrogation, allucinations n all that glorious jazz.'

'She's trippin?'

'To la-la land n back again.'

'How long does it last?'

'Fuck knows. She might be right fer tea.' He paused. 'This all look familiar to yer?'

'What you mean?' I said.

'Well, oo did yer nab it off?'

'You don't wanna know.'

'Yer may be right but av still gotta know.'

'You know that Formby's club burnt down last night?'

'Burnt down?' he said. 'What club?'

'You need to get out more, Trevor. Into the world. It's eighty-five degrees – mad hot out there.'

'Bollocks.'

'Get a tan.'

Stark came back with the glass of water for Tara.

I said: 'Make sure that one doesn't go back to bed.' Stark nodded.

'D'you have a phone here?' I said.

Trevor showed me his serious face. 'Downstairs. Behind the couch. Leave it ow yer found it when yer finished.'

'Off the hook,' I said, glancing back at Tara. 'You

wanna get one o them mobiles, mate. Better for business.'

'I fuckin don't,' he said.

Gemma had been wrong. It wasn't coke her Den had been shifting down at the Kitchen Club. It was this. The question was who'd given it him. And then which bugger's toes had he stepped on to get his club card revoked. Or maybe he'd just pinched a bone from a bigger dog's bowl.

I found Trevor's house phone showing under one of the pancake sofa cushions and gave Gerry's number another go. It rang and rang but still no joy.

11

FAVOURS

I PUT THE phone down and picked it up again. I called an old mate's work number.

'Razdan's Garage, Rusholme.'

'Is Maz about?' I said.

'Who this?'

'Tell um it's Bane.'

'. . .'

I waited. I could hear them shouting, rattling in the yard.

'. . . Bane, ow's it goin?'

'Alright, mate. You?'

'Notsabad.'

'How's your sister?'

'Fuck off – nah, she's alright, yeah.'

'You got a lot on this afternoon?' I said.

'Bitsnbobs. Be poppin out in a bit, though. What yer need doin?'

'Need you to look at the motor. I've got cracks in the front bumper and some fuckin scrapes above the wheel arch.'

'Shit, mate. Ow yer manage that?'

'Last night – cab driver on Deansgate. Took the paint off.'

Maz laughed in my ear.

'Was one o yours,' I said.

'Nah, yer mean a bloody rag ed?' he laughed. 'They want sendin back on the next banana boat ome.'

'Can you get it done for Monday?'

'Wednesday. *Next* Wednesday. Yer want us to vac it fer yer n all?'

'Champion, mate.'

'. . . Ah said to im right, "where's yer papers?" N ee went, "ere." Passed us a driver's licence. N am lookin at the picture n it's me bloody cousin Shy!' Maz said.

'Him with the transport firm?' I said.

Maz nodded at me, impressed. 'Aye, that's the one.'

'The snidey bastard. How'd he get hold of it?'

This was Razdan's Garage. We stood by my car out in the big yard. Junk parts piled up like a gypo's wet dream. Petrol fumes distorting the hot air above uneven tarmac. Somebody's Lamborghini Diablo blocking a rusty electric roller-shutter.

'Fuck knows.' Maz crouched down next to the wheel

and ran some chubby fingers along the scratched paintwork.

'He do a runner?' I said.

'Off like a whippet. But the boys found im in a shisha bar, Wednesday night. Let's jus say they ad a word.'

I'd met Maz when we were both sixteen. He'd moved to England. Then to Wythie. I'd been chasing after this gorgeous bird with hair all down her back, eyes like Guinness. I'd just started getting somewhere when she turned out to be his sister. Their dad owned a hardware shop in Civic before he sold it to club in with the family's mechanic firm and pushed out to town. He had her working the till on Saturday mornings. I used to go in the shop after ordering my old man's dinner at the chippy next door, just to get a look in. When Maz found out a white feller was diddling his older sis, he lamped me across Painswick Park. He was a big lad, six-two, even then. All flab but the weight's what counts. I remember waking up face down in a puddle with a loose molar. Mates ever since.

Maz stood up and said to me: 'Bumper's ready to drop. But nowt this, really. A buff-up job. It's jus gettin round to it.'

I shielded my eyes from the sun and went round to the boot and opened it. I called him over. 'You got anywhere cool I could put this?'

'Bane, mate. Yer know ah don't touch the sauce.'

'Shame. You know anyone who'll shift it?'

He blew air out of his lips and his fat cheeks ballooned. 'Shameful, son. What yer think I am?'

'A whisky man,' I said. 'Six bottles of Glenmorangie. Courtesy of Frank's friends at the Cash n Carry.'

'Yer still knockin about wiv Frank's crew, then?'

'Yeah,' I said.

'Yer sure?'

'Yeah, why? What've you heard?'

'Nowt.'

Maz looked down at the booze, sighed and shut the boot. 'We'll tek it inside n av anuva look.'

Next Wednesday became this Monday after three.

When Maz was younger, some uncle caught him hoovering lines in the spare room, a blondie called Sharon from round the way stuck to his lap. The parents packed his bags the following week, sent him back home. But he'd turned up again four years ago, still a rum bugger.

Maz carried the booze into the office. There was a girl at a desk, singing down the phone in Urdu.

'Alright, love,' I said to her.

She smiled back, still singing.

Maz put the booze away and pulled out two cardboard boxes stacked next to a filing cabinet. He snapped them open. There was foreign writing all down the side.

The girl said: 'Oi! Hands!' – trapping the phone against her neck.

'Ay?' Maz turned his head.

'Get your oily grubby hands off the stock.'

'Calm down!' he said. Then to me: 'What appened to yer jacket?'

'RIP,' I went.

'Yud rinsed it to fuck, mate. Ee-ah, tek a look yerself. It's top gear this. Yer ad one o these, dint yer?'

I pulled out a crushed red Harrington. Not a G9 Original but it might do for now.

Maz said: 'Kam, love – where's the rest?'

The bird put the phone down and stood up. She was slim with a big chest and no arse. She pointed at a third box under the far desk in the corner.

'What colours?' I said.

Maz said: 'What colour yer after?'

'Let's have a look.'

Maz showed me a hatchback through the office window and said: 'Al lend yer this fer weekend. Keys are in.'

'Cheers.'

'Was yer in town las night?' he said as we walked back out. There was a cassette radio on the sunroof of a Volvo 940. R. Kelly and Aaliyah echoed through the unit.

'Yeah,' I said.

'See it appen?'

'What, the fire? Yeah. Fuckin mad round Deansgate. Told you – how I ended up with that.'

'Oh aye,' he said.

'*You* see it?'

'Ah were round our way.'

'What's that Diablo after?' I said. 'New plates?'

Maz laughed. 'Maybe.'

I opened my car up.

'Yer forget summat?'

'Somethin I need out the glovebox,' I said, shutting the passenger door again and passing him the keys.

I'd left one of the bricks back with Trevor and wrapped the other one in a Kwik Save bag and taken it with me. I stuffed it inside my new Harrington and drove off in my courtesy chariot up Oxford Road.

12

CANAL STREET

I STOOD INSIDE a crowd, listening to some of it, and some of it was priceless.

'Ee's never ad any fanny.'

'Fanny? Ee's never even felt a tit.'

'Bet ee's always felt a tit.'

'Yeah. Ee's bloody bent as a two-bob note, im.'

'Too fuckin right. Dunt know it yet, though. Bless im.'

Our Gordon's not a fan. He can't be doing with them. But I've no problem with puffters, me. I'm not mithered. And there was one I still needed to find.

The Village. The mucky canal blistered in the sun. There were plenty – faffing about in the street – pale skinny denims, tops off, catching tans. Teenagers to old blokes. A few lezzers. Bickering. Bitching. All having a drink, a gossip and a giggle. I took my jacket off. Nobody eyed me up.

I walked down a bit and found a place with some younger lads outside. They sat necking Hooch under the umbrellas and I went through the doors and up to the bar. Behind it – a bony white face and orange cap-sleeved T-shirt said: 'Ay-up, some eye candy, Roger.'

'Alright,' I said.

He went: 'We don't do pints, love.'

'Not after a pint.'

'Wiv finished lunch.'

'I'm not after lunch,' I said. 'I'm after a word.'

'Steady, love! Ear this one, Roger? Wants a word.'

'You know a Gerry that might come in ere?'

'Pardon?'

'The lad's name. Gerry.'

'Gerry?'

'A young lad. Bout this high. Twenny. Spiky blond hair.'

'N ee comes in ere?'

'I dunno. Does he?'

'Roger, love?'

This was going to be hard work.

Roger turned around, took his hat off and folded tattooed arms on the bar top. There was a sweaty crease across his forehead where the cap had been.

'Ee's after some young lad called Gerry,' the first bartender went.

'Gerry?' Roger said.

He went: 'That's what ah jus said!'

'Well?' I said. 'You two know the lad, or what?'

'Nah . . .' they said together.

'Any idea where I could ask about?'

'Ow should we know?'

'Well, you two Marys've been useless.'

'Cheeky beggar.' The first one smiled.

'Try the Union,' Roger said. 'If yer fancy joinin. N yull get a cold pint there if yer lucky.'

She was forty-odd, white, scrawny in a string-vest top, haircut – a number three all-round. Thin lips stopped chewing gum and she leant forward over the counter while still pulling a draught. She stared at my shoes and then crawled her way up, looking through me until we were eye-to-eye. She said: 'What yer avin, naff – n Irn-Bru?'

The Union stank of perfume and cigs. It wasn't busy in – most of them were out there in the sun.

A Western was ending on the telly up on the wall behind the bar. A Gary Cooper.

I asked Number Three if she knew a Gerry.

'No idea. But a young lad? Ee won't be a regular in ere.'

I had the bastard number when I needed the bastard address. But was this the best I could think of? This was a dead-end.

'What's on the jukebox?' I said, pointing to it across the pub.

'It's packed up,' she said.

'It probably got sick o playin Kylie.'

She almost smiled. 'Then "Paint It Black"'s what did it . . . Yud be surprised.'

Two Marys came through the main doors, one shouting into his mobile while the other one asked Number Three for another round.

I watched a short feller with too much hair slide out of an empty booth and mince up to the bar. 'Yer comin mine?' he said to the queer on the phone, a Cheshire-Cat grin with a dead front tooth. He wasn't young.

The other one took the mobile from his ear and went: 'Yer must av sunstroke. Go yours? Why?'

'Av twelve inches, a jacuzzi n a bagawhizz.'

The other young lad paid for the round and chipped in: 'Twelve-inch telly, yer mean. Ee lives on Hodder Square, this one. Talks absolute bollocks.'

They were both howling. The one with a mobile gave Black Tooth's shoulder a poke. The poor bastard looked mortified: 'Well both o yers can get fucked!'

The two lads walked back outside with their round.

I said: 'Nowt worse than bein shot down.'

'Worse in ere of a night,' he said to me.

'I bet.'

'Ow bout you, love? Avin one?'

'No, ta.'

He sighed and sat on the next stool and put his hands together on the bar like he was saying his prayers. The local news was on the box now. He said: 'There any musicals on, Cynth? Depressin fuck outta me, this is.'

Cynth poured a short rum and coke as she looked across to the telly: 'Ah can't work it – wiv lost the bloody remote.'

97

'Can you work the sound, love?' I said. 'The button on the side.'

'Ang on. Ere, chin up.' She pushed the drink into his hands.

'Ow much?' he said.

'Nowt.'

'Cheers. No fool like n old fool is there?'

She went over to the telly and had a play.

. . . twenty-one, gunned down in his home last night between the hours of eleven p.m. and two a.m. Greater Manchester Police are making enquiries and are urging residents and visitors of Sanworth Close, Ardwick, to come forward with any information regar—

The screen flipped onto Yul Brynner – all singing, all dancing. Debbie Kerr floating about the place in a daft ballgown.

'Ere we go,' Cynth went. 'We're not doin too bad after all.'

Back outside. The puff was gabbing on his mobile again. I pinched it off him with a shove – not hard – but the way he fell you'd think he was after a penalty. His mate watched, did nowt.

'Ay!'

'Ay!'

'Ay you!'

'Ay!'

They all piped together, feet glued still as I walked through the crowd.

'That's a bloke in pattern tights,' I said, pointing with my free hand.

'Tis yeah,' someone said. 'Now fuck off!'

I stabbed each number in with my thumb slowly from memory – I wasn't too good with these mobiles. It rang and rang and then somebody on the other end said hello. Third time unlucky.

'Is this Gerry?' I went.

'Who's calling?' There was plenty going on in the background. Voices. Shuffling around.

'Is this Gerry?' I said again. I was too late.

'There has been a serious incident at this residence. I need your name and details, sir. I'm a duty officer at the scene.'

I ended the call and smashed the mobile up against the brick side of a puff's bar. The cover spun back – helicoptered off the short drop into the canal. I stopped, looked at the circuit board in the gutter. I caught my breath and walked off, embarrassed.

13

ME WANDERIN MEMRY NOW FERSAKES

A SQUASHED ROW of houses ran up both sides of Sanworth Close with a local at the top end. The pigs were still about – they'd taped up the gate, were ducking in and out of a blue tent in the front plot. There were neighbours watching, gabbing in a line at their front doors. They hissed at their kids to come inside.

> . . . Abdul Muhsi, chief suspect-at-large in the Safir Hassan murder investigation, has yet to be found. Authorities believe he may attempt to leave Britain, with security forces at major airports being placed on high alert. Among those keeping vigilant . . .

I switched the radio off, took the keys and headed down the road.

I walked a few doors past the house of horrors. The boys in blue nattering into chest radios.

'Messy job, this,' one said. 'A right do. Thorough as fuck.'

Further down, a few young kids were playing footy against somebody's wall.

'Oi,' I whistled to a white lad of about ten, dribbling by the kerb. His head flicked up and he passed the ball to his mate and came over.

'You know what happened over there?' I said, pointing at the pigs.

'Tell im to get stuffed!' another lad shouted.

'Shudup!' the boy said back. 'Yeh. This queer what got killed. Fuckin shot im.'

'He was a whatsit?' I said.

'Ee was a fuckin queerboy, we seen im. Ant we lads!? We ad, mister.'

'Who did it?'

'They dunno. But our kid saw a dock-off van drivin up street.'

'What was his name? The queer.'

'Gerry Carson.'

I gave him a quid.

Unlocking the motor.

'Like pissin vultures, you lot!' A tubby woman was shouting, wagging her sovereign finger at me, behind her front gate. 'Wiv ad anuff o yer terday. Ah won't be readin *Evenin News* no more.'

As if I looked like a fucking journalist.

She said: 'What yer want wiv me kids? Jus nosey?'
'Aren't we all?' I got back in the car.

The only bugger I knew of who'd left the Kitchen Club on Tuesday night, with Alice, with Safir, was now as dead as them. That big black van had seen some action last night. Gemma's. The club. Now Gerry. A sweet hat-trick. Somebody's hit list.

It had gone nine – still light. Still pretty warm. I'd been driving round for a good hour, windows down, radio up – cheating on Biggie – 2Pac on the go. I was grinding my teeth, having another little think. Just who the fuck was this Lance? Who took those smutty photos that went in the fire? And who was the lucky tosser that was in them?

The McVitie's factory was coming up on my left. The smell of biscuits dead sickly in the heat.

I pulled over by the flowers, pissing off more foreign cabbies using the bus lane. There was a droopy bouquet sellotaped round a lamppost. A big card stuck on, flapping with the passing traffic.

alice you use to look so nice our kid in yellow
so i thought you woud like some yellow carnashuns
you always looked stuning babes im going to bring some
more to the funeral im saving for an even bigger bunch
i wish you had just come to me ive lost my bloody
bezzy mate from school our trentons growing hes nearly
twelv remember when u use to baby sit?
will always miss u love
Jan
xxx

This is where she'd been found. Where the bastards had dumped her, sped off in a 7-Series bimmer and left me and the pigs still scratching our heads. Not that they could give a shit. They had bigger fish to fry than my Alice. They were pissing in international waters. Safir.

Safir the fuckin sex monster. Just wait till them tabloids get wind.

And then there was the bombing. Poor Alice. Two whopping great spotlight stealers – or legit excuses for the plod to give even less of a fuck. Cue violins. A fiddler busking on Market Street would do.

It seemed like square one. Just a different square one. But it was either this or go back to town. Back to Frank.

Dusk. Otterburn Close, Hulme. The place smelled like a bad barbecue. I parked up next to a toasted Cortina. Some monged-out gypo, on one, was standing in the mouth of a throughway just ahead, in his bed vest, button trackies and cap. My headlights wiped him as he swayed up to the car before I flicked the engine off. His fists were up, legs wide, like he thought he was ten men. I took the steering lock out of the footwell, opened the driver door and showed it him. He fucked off. There was just something about this shithole that wanted a piece of me. But I wasn't getting mugged tonight.

The red steering lock was a heavy steel bar, a corkscrew fit for the column. You could do some serious damage with these things. It was all I could use it for because I couldn't find Maz's key for it anywhere. I put it through the wheel to make it look like it was locked, got out and went for a wander.

KELZO REIGNS 94

. . . Mad graffiti along the underpass – acid colours, angry shapes. A dog barked but no one seemed to be about. I came out onto the second green. It was a car graveyard. There was one bloke spray-tagging a caravan – this black girl with a bald head behind him. She was hopping over a chucked sofa.

More dog barks in the distance.

He finished the graffiti, called her over and they went off up one of the open stairwells.

It was soon dark.

The papers said Safir's body had been found underneath rubble in the basement. But this place didn't really have a working basement. The bottom-floor flats were damp, rotting away – a few scumbags had knocked through two empty ones at the back – probably using the space to have a rave, sell gear, or just squat for a while. The body had been hidden underneath one of the fallen breeze-block walls. She hadn't died here, they'd said. She'd been put here. The pigs had marked it with posters tacked to the columns outside, appealing for information. On them – the same photo that had been fed to the press – Safir the champagne sipper, the one I'd seen on the *Evening News*'s front page back on Thursday at Frank's. I dragged the blue-and-white tape away from a box window missing the glass but it was too dark to climb through and have a kick around inside. I should have come down sooner.

A dog yapped. Closer now. There was a big gang of kids, maybe twenty-odd, heading up the walk in my direction. Some on bikes, some on foot, all ages, all sizes – and from what I could see of their mugs, mostly lads. A couple of them were waving torches in the dark. There were two bull terriers thrashing on the leash in front. I kept still, my back against the wall, wishing I'd brought that steering lock.

One lad pedalled out ahead, a small white lad on a girl's scuffed-up mountain bike.

'Jacob,' I said.

The brake pads squeaked. The bike was a bit too big for him.

'You remember us?' I said.

'Yeah.'

'What's with all this?'

A black lad rode up and pulled off his hood. He was taller and a bit older than Jacob. 'The hunt,' he said.

'We fuckin got owt!?' Somebody behind said.

None of these voices had broken yet.

'Nah, Knuckles jus got a rat.' The black lad said, looking at the dog and then at the Witch's boy. 'Oo's ee?'

'I'm a good mate o Jacob's,' I said.

'Got any fags?'

Knuckles, or the other one, had flanked me in a second. Thick stub tail in the air, this giant silver head, mostly mouth, sniffing up my trousers, breathing sheer noise.

'Ee dunt mind yer, seems. What's ee like, ay? Usually ee'll jus av yer.'

One of his big paws was digging into the toe of my right shoe. I bit my tongue. He looked up at me, wet eyes – after grub.

Jacob said: 'Knuckles. Down.'

He did as he was told and sat for a moment but there was too much going on for him to stay still for long. Most of the gang swarmed round in a wide half-circle but those with torches seemed to have fucked off. The ones left were just shadows. Five-foot and under.

'This your lot?' I said to Jacob.

He nodded blankly. Eyes hollowed black.

The other lad came forward again and grinned down at Knuckles. 'Gunna get im t'tear up fuckin tabbies, mate.'

'Nah. D'yer wanna not, mate? Ah mean what's the fuckin point?' Another kid said from the gloom.

'Nah, fuck you, mate,' he said.

'S'not what we're after. That int the hunt.'

The black lad held his chin up. 'This fucker mard or what? Yer bein a mardarse.'

'That int the hunt, mate!' Another shadow joined in from the back.

Then from a distance: 'Wiv fuckin got us one! Come on!'

They sounded it out in a sequence from across the green like a foghorn game of Chinese Whispers.

They were off.

Knuckles barked, barging through sets of legs. He knocked one lad off his bike, dragging the young kid with the leash onto his knees before he could let the monster loose.

Jacob had stayed.

He said: 'Come and watch us.'

I asked him why.

There were faulty floodlights brightening up the trash-heaps at the top end of the lot, round the side of the green. Two out of twelve garages looked firebombed. A row of six either side. A couple of them had been painted-up by our distinguished KELZO. Signed, local talent.

They chased it to a collapsed passage between two garages. None of the kids could squeeze through but Knuckles scrambled over the crush of torn bin bags and ferreted it back out.

The other bullie made the kill, a brown bitch that looked yellow when it dashed under the light. She shook it, using her weight to bring it down first.

It didn't bark or howl. It made this weird bubbly whine like a Walkman running low on Duracells – but even over the whine, I heard the bones snapping.

'Let's get on it,' one kid went.

'Fuckin av it,' someone else said.

But it wasn't over quick for the poor bugger. The

dogs had a play with it, and when a back leg was torn off, Knuckles and the bitch fought over it, bloody great jaws foaming goz. A right din. Then they chased each other off, two docked tails wagging for more blood.

The black lad was first to give it a poke. He nudged the furry back with his foot but the life was still draining out of its missing leg and his white Reeboks got covered in blood.

'Thema fucked, mate,' said this weedy kid with a Stanley knife.

'Shit,' he said, lifting his leg up.

The weedy lad knelt down and stuck the blade in its belly and stabbed his way down, cutting it to ribbons. 'Look at them guts! Fuckin ell – it's proper angin!'

'Rank!' a girl said.

'Giz that torch a minute,' he went, his arm held out, looking like a piece of white cotton dangling from the sleeve of his T-shirt.

'Nah,' some lad with a torch said. 'Gotta get us anuva one, mate.'

Somehow, it was like they'd been after one of their own. A little scrappy victim – scared, mucky, mangy, battered – after a decent handout. Just surviving. Just trying to get by.

Jacob came forward and took the Stanley knife away from the weedy lad. It looked massive in his hands. He bent down and started to saw off the fox's head from the throat back. It took him nearly a minute. He lifted the head up high and they all cheered like kiddies at

Old Trafford. Then Jacob walked down two garages and blooded the next tatty door. Number Eight.

'You finished, Jake?' I said.

He nodded.

He chucked the severed head onto the flat roof of the garage. He picked up the rest of the fox with one hand and lifted his mountain bike. He dangled the carcass between the bars and hopped on.

I moved the car round. It hadn't even been keyed.

Alone.

Garage number Eight. Tatty up-and-over door, dripping warm fox blood.

I pushed Maz's steering lock through a hole already in the middle-right of the door and forced it wider. I forced the lock catch inside until a bracket gave out and then leant my weight at the top so I could get some clearance at the bottom. Tracks so rusty the door stuttered open, sounded painful. The handle came off the axle, mid-lift.

Darkness. A battery lamp was roped up, hanging from the ceiling. I switched it on and the lamp fizzed and swung. Wooden shelves with old paint tins ran down both walls of the garage. I shut the door behind me but kept it wedged open with the biggest tin. The place was chalky dry and stank of oil. There was a workbench in the middle with a hacksaw waiting on top. I blew the metal filings onto a white floor sheet spread out over something against the back wall. Underneath the sheet were three black sports holdalls.

I unzipped the first – a soft baby-blue towel inside, slick and stained with oil. The towel had a tree emblem on it with writing stitched below. It belonged to some posh Cheshire gym and health spa. I peeled back the towel to get a look at the shooters.

Sub-fucking-machine guns. I held one up to the lamp, a serial number – model name: *MP5 9mm*. It wasn't as heavy as a shotgun – this surprised me.

I slid it back in the bag and pulled out a larger shooter: *Crvena Zastava M70*. More foreign writing was engraved up the barrel and stock, a tally count carved into the butt, the same with the rest of them. I shut my left eye and aimed with the sight: a paint tin on the shelf, third from the end. I held my breath. My legs nearly went. These were scary customers. I pointed rifle to floor and had a breather. When I'd sorted myself out, I tried the next bag – packed full again, guns like sardines in a tin. The third was stuffed with fancy gear – silencers, flash suppressors, ammunition. Each bag had its own oiled-up health-spa rag keeping the rust off the merch for the time being.

Only two would fit in the boot, the last bag had to go on the backseat. The white floor sheet kept our Maz's upholstery in decent nick.

By the time I reached Ancoats I was spooked. I'd clocked three black Transits along the way – one in the rear-view, the other had coasted up next to me at a T-junction, and the last was parked up outside a Sue Ryder's on Swan Street.

Back in May, Frank asked us to put the fear into this bugger who still owed him a few bob from the year before. He'd been grassed up to Frank after he squared a debt for three-and-a-half grand with another Great White. This flat was the quietest: just vacant factory space for a quarter-mile round. The whole poxy floor and even the floor below were empty. So we took him up here to help readjust his finances, divvy up this new fortune a bit fairer – after all, Frank was due his return. It turned out this bloke's old man had just gone and he'd left him a classic motor to flog. Since that day, I'd held onto the flat keys.

There were still curled-up pages from the *Mirror* on the floor, blood-soaked black, starchy. The poor bastard. *Somebody bring me back some money, please,* Frank had said. I chucked the newspapers, put the fold-up dining chair where it belonged, nylon rope still knotted to the back. All this with the big light off. Grim reminders. But the flat was nearer than home. Maybe safer now as well. Our Frank had six of these little hideaways dotted around Manny but we were only supposed to know about four of them. It wasn't glamorous but it did the job. These were rent-free gaffs, no frills. Sorted. And most of the time the flats were just handy. For some of the lads, a cab back here with a bird from town was cheaper than a cab back home. But they usually had to mither Frank for the keys – catch him in a good mood.

Now there was a bag of shooters stuffed upright in the airing cupboard. Another behind the bed. I'd fed the last lot under the floorboards – along with a good few ton of Den's money – one at a time. There was a cut-away piece of skirting board, and the gap was just big enough.

So they were stashing their tools right under the dragon's wing. I wondered how many more of these stockpiles there were. A top-of-the-range arsenal imported to Otterburn fucking Close? Daft or brilliant? It didn't matter now. What did matter:

If they already knew I'd fucked off with the lot.

If they were coming for me.

I tilted the Venetians and put the big light on. I pulled out the sports bag from behind the bed again and had a root through the side pocket. A couple of balaclavas. I remembered the gear.

Burundanga?

I took it out of my Harrington, got undressed, slipped the magic brick behind the loose skirting and crawled onto the bed with a dock-off gun the size of Jacob.

From my pillow, I watched the front door all night. I watched it with two eyes, then with one. But somehow I slept.

Then it started with a big bang. Still dark. Sounded like Beirut. Bastards pounding the door in. I fell onto the floor, scrambled to the window. A fucking van across the street. I squinted hard, wiping wet from my eyes before I looked back into the flat. The alarm clock bled 05.37. Red digits with tails.

Bang.

I rubbed bleary eyes again.

Bang. Bang.

I went for the gun as they broke the door in.

There was a flash of wide shapes — two, three of them, more. And then out of nowhere I was on my arse. A few brick-fist wallops made sure I was down for good.

14

ME DAD

I FELT MY face back on the pillow. Right temple throbbing but nothing numb – maybe nothing broken.

'Ah barely touched yer. Gettin soft, you.'

'What time is it?' I said, opening my eyes. We were alone in the flat. The two of us.

'Gone six. Yer bin out of it fer ages. We put yer to bed. Puff. Sides, me knuckles int even skinned.' He held his fist up but it was still too dark to see.

'You decked us like fuckin Akinwande,' I said.

'Akin-wanday? Now there's an enry that int soft as a woolly woofter. That Williams fight las munf? Ah knew ee'd fuckin av im.' The words were same old Gordon, but I could hear the rage under them. Cold. Livid.

'I'm still seein stars.'

'Bane, yer courtin at the moment?' His voice was low.

'Ay?'

'This to do wiv a bird, yeah? Like, yer know – a proper one.'

Alice.

'No,' I said.

He was slouching on a dining chair by the foot of the bed. He tapped the back pages of a newspaper in his hands and then grinned up at me. 'What the fuck's all this, then? Idin out? Yer in a bit ova state, mate, int yer lad?'

'What do you want?'

He tried a smirk but he was still stewing. 'Could do wiv a brew n a biccy if one's goin.'

'Not been shoppin, mate.'

'Av seen. Got nowt stashed anywhere?'

'There's somebody's gin in the back o the sink cupboard. But that's about it.'

'Gordon's?' he said.

'Very good.'

'Nice one.' Gordon folded the newspaper and tossed it on the floor.

'That today's?' I said.

'Yesterday's,' he went, heading for the kitchenette.

I sat up. Daylight was starting to find its way through the blinds. 'Where the lads?' I said.

'Sent um ome wiv a few quid to keep um quiet. Mek out we still ant found yer yet. Frank'll be fucked off but most of us av angovers. Includin us. Ah dint preciate this, mate. It comin to this.'

'Good one last night was it?'

Gordon came back over with the bottle. His frown became a grin. 'Oh aye – yer missed a right one las night, mate. Saturdays are a fuckin giggle.'

'Cop off?'

He took a fat swig of Gordon's Gin and wiped his mouth with the back of his arm. He talked slowly again, like he was sick of it all. 'Us? Scored yeah, but she were nowt to write ome bout. Fuck it. Fanny's fanny, av always said. Shut yer eyes n yer shaggin oo yer wannabe shaggin.' He was dead upset about all this and he couldn't hide it. 'Yer sure this int to do wiv a bird?' he said.

'Not like *you* mean,' I said.

He slammed the gin bottle down on the bedside table, kept his fingers round the neck. The table legs wobbled. His brick-fist white. 'Is this it, then? What wiv bin waitin fer? Are yer pissed?' he spat, his face up in mine.

'I'd never touch gin.'

'Yer think ah fuckin preciate bein made to come round ere at alf-five in mornin – on a Sunday! N we ad to find yer first. We trashed yer ouse. Frank's orders. Ee's fumin! Ee wants yer in a bloody box. Yuv bin a silly cunt, Bane. Yer don't forget bout Frank. We got in this together, me n you, knob ed! Now av a bit o fuckin respect.'

'Sit down.'

We squared for a moment before he did as he was told, taking the bottle with him.

'I'm sorry,' I said.

He looked at the floor. The sun was rising – shining stronger on him by the minute. I got off the bed and went to the window. There was still a black van parked outside. A sticker on the side said *Dave D. Mobile DJ*.

I turned back to Gordon: 'When the fuck did Frank get so shirty bout time keepin? I've not clocked in for a couple o days. So what?'

'Never done fuck all like it before. If yer on payroll yer on the job. N ee dunt like bein ignored.'

'Me n you, alright, though?' I said.

Our Gordon nodded. 'Yeah.'

'I'm not larkin about here for nothin.'

'Best not be fer nowt. Ah knew yer wunt be but still – awkward do now, this. Awkward do. Bitin and that feeds if ah don't bring yer to the King battered to fuck like ee wants.'

'I need you, Gordon, mate.'

'It's what we do. It's what *I* do. This is what ah do.'

'Breakfast?' I said.

He sighed. Yawned. 'Could do wiv a butty.'

I said: 'Let's go get some scran.'

Gordon cocked his head. 'So what's wiv all the fuckin shooters?'

Edna's Caff. Wythie. Condiments lined up on the red plastic tables. It was a trek, but it was good to be back on home turf.

Adam and the Ants – 'Never Trust a Man with Egg on His Face' chugged out from the radio on the counter.

Not bad, but it was a bit loud for this time of the morning.

'Nowt like a brew,' Gordon said. 'Gaspin.'

'Not heard this in time,' I said.

'Oo is it?'

'Adam Ant,' I said.

Gordon pulled a face. 'Used to flog all this shite wiv yer old man dint yer?'

'Salt?'

'Ta.' He smothered his bacon, sausage, fried egg and hash brown sarnie with the stuff. Lifted it up for a monster bite.

Adam was off. 80s Costello next. Too much to ask for a bit of hip-hop in here, but this was harmless enough. I tucked into my scrambled on toast and realised I'd missed this little place. 'So how's your old man?' I said. 'Still ill?'

'Ill? Ee's fuckin right as rain. That's the problem.'

'You wanna get your own place. You're a big lad now.'

'Don't start again.'

'I'm not.'

'What we gunna do bout Frank?' he said.

'We'll sort that when we have to. I've gotta see this through.'

Gordon pointed a greasy finger at my Harrington draped over the next chair: 'Thought yer lost that in the Kitchen barbecue on Friday?'

'Maz sorted us a new one.'

'Bloody Rupert bloody Bear, you. Must jus av a wardrobe full o same bastard outfit.'

'I'm always a damn sight sharper than you, son.'

'Fuck off,' he chewed. 'Bein flash means nowt.'

I let it go. He swallowed.

'Where is ee?' he said.

I looked up. 'He's here now.'

The caff door chimed and then shuddered to.

'How we doin, Vic?' I said. 'Much on?'

He came over. 'Work's bin appallin. Bloody shockin, enry. Pakis, piss eds n puffters in backseat. All night, every night.'

I said: 'Glad you're well.'

Gordon said: 'Sit down, yer miserable get.'

'Sandy! Tea when yer ready, cot,' he shouted over to the counter – pulling up the chair next to Gordon and lighting a fag.

'In a jiffy, Vic,' Sandy went.

Vic was wearing his tweed trilby with the soggy rim and a tatty charity-shop Crombie. Gordon's dad was only sixty-two this year. He looked like an anorexic Father Christmas.

'Bin to the bookies fer us?' he said to Gordon.

'Dint av time yesterday.'

'Al give yer time.' He clipped Gordon's ear, back-handed. Once. Twice. The brute didn't flinch. Vic always blamed his bad shoulder on our Gordon.

Gordon said: 'Anyroad, ow come *you* dint? What was yer doin yesterday?'

'Never yer mind.' He turned to me: 'Ad a coloured in the back, other day, Enry. Bloody ell. Wanted radio up. Ah said yer can fuck off.'

'What did he want on?' I said.

'Jungle bungle bollocks. Not Sammy. If it'd bin Sammy — now that would've bin bloody different.'

'I see.'

'Then ee tried to say ah were chargin im time n alf. Tight bastards some of um, yer know. These foreign beggars. Tight as a duck's arse.'

'Right.'

He hissed at Gordon. 'N you, son! Yer neeva nowt ner summat, you. Sat there wiv yer muscles thinkin yer bloody Conan — yer a bloody villain. Yer wanna get yerself a real job. Ooligan is what yah.'

Gordon's chest heaved. He pushed his empty plate away. 'Fuckin leave it, Dad.'

'N that's me ouse that is that yer left a state. Yer jus pay board.'

'Ah pay the fuckin rent, ah do.'

'Fuck off, yer do.'

'Ee-ah,' Sandy said, putting a brew in front of Vic.

'Ta, cot,' he said.

She took our finished plates away and sauntered back to the counter.

'The arse on that. Would yer shag it?' Vic went.

'Aye, ad do er,' Gordon said with a nod. 'That's a nine, that.'

'Steady, son.'

They traded wily smirks, pushed their matching bum chins out. Thick as thieves. They looked over at me.

'Well,' Vic went. 'Would yer?'

I rubbed my sore temple. I laughed and laughed.

Iceland car park, across the road from Edna's Caff. Vic lifted the boot of his taxi, wincing at his bad shoulder.

I said: 'Seems like everybody's at it these days.'

'Bollocks,' Vic said.

'Tidy operation, knock-off. You must do alright.'

'This is nowt, this. Dunt even go as far as tips. Good gear, though. Do yer fer life this. Quality stuff. Now what yer after?'

'The works.'

'Even fer this daft-lookin gym munkey?'

Gordon seethed.

Vic went: 'Ee-ah, got two nice Fred Perrys, got designer joggers, got two pairs o latest Adeedus . . . n some o them weight gloves. This'll be right this. Flash as fuck.'

Gordon tore open the shrink-wrap with his teeth and flapped out a white polo XL. 'Got any Lonsdale?' he said.

Vic slapped his ear: 'Oi, meat ed, they don't wear that stuff at the posh ones. Do they bloody eck. Sides, yer got that tatty shite at ome. This is what yer want.'

He went: 'Alright, ow much?'

Vic pulled down the wavy rim of his trilby. 'Seventy fer the lot.'

'Yer can fuck right off – robbin bastard!' Gordon said. He chucked the Fred Perry back in the boot after getting a third clip round the ear.

'Fifty-five,' Vic said to me.

'Twenty-five,' I said, picking out a black polo.

He dropped his spent fag on the tarmac, padded his shabby Crombie for the next one. 'Thirty quid,' he said. 'Tek the lot n sod off.'

Boom. Flutter. With both windows down in the courtesy chariot, we heard the gunshots. I was easing off the pedal just north of Macclesfield. Barley fields on the left of the A-road. Scraps of forest to the right. Badger roadkill ahead.

'They're idin in there,' our Gordon said as we stopped at a roundabout. He pointed his arm out of the window to the barley fields: 'What they after?'

'Dunno,' I said, 'Thought it was just clay pigeon round here.'

'They should let um av a go in Civic.'

Boom. We craned our necks and saw the birds scatter through the sunroof.

'Or at me dad,' Gordon said. 'Ee could do wiv a fuckin cartridge up the backside.'

'Your Dad's alright, y'know, Gordon.'

'Coffin-dodgin ol bugger swat ee is. Looks right fer the scrap eep already.'

'Now, now.'

'Member me first love? Debs.'

'Debra?' I said.

'Yeah.'

'Did I know you that far back?'

'Course yer fuckin knew us. Debs. Debra!

Sweet-sixteen. Feather-cut. Big arse. Yer bloody pinched er off us in the end.'

'Oh aye, yeah. You'd had enough though, you said.'

'First fuckin date, yeah? Ah took er t'pictures, Oxford Road. Gory slasher, it were. Debs were jittery as fuck. Squirmin in er seat, yellin out, shuttin er eyes, missin all the best bits.'

'She'd yell out?'

'"Ee's behind yer, missus!" Honest t'God. Daft cow. Then she ends up walkin out, sez she's ad enough. So we leave, right – alfway through – n she flags a taxi in street. Guess oo pulls in?'

'Ol Victor Payne?'

'Aye! It's only me fuckin dad! Ee were a black-cabbie man in them days, member? So we get in n ee's at it, "Where to, cot? Ours or yours?" Debs dunt know what t'think. Then ee's chargin me fer the ride. We get to ers n it turns out ah dint av enough. Ah thought we was gunna be busin it back. Me dad wants the muney n we're jus at it, right – so am bout t'bash im then our Debs fuckin pays. She jus pays!'

'What you complainin about?' I said.

'Ee showed us up.'

'He's your dad. It's his fuckin job.'

Gordon rolled up the passenger window, his other big paw tapping the dash. 'Mate, dunno bout you but am gunna get a fuckin sweat on in there. Av not benched in time.'

'We've gotta get in there, first.'

I turned off the A-road and we passed a black road

sign with gold writing. Splats of bird shit covered the same tree emblem I'd seen on the towels.

The Florencia
Fitness Centre & Health Spa
PRIVATE LAND

'This it?' Gordon said, taking his seatbelt off.

'Guess so, mate. Get the shooter.' I flicked the rear-view.

'We tekin it in wiv us?' Gordon reached for the sports holdall on the backseat, now crammed with Vic's cheap knock-off kit and one of the loaded MP5s. He lugged it over the seats and wedged the bag in the footwell against his leg. He patted the top end. Grinned. 'Right fuckin mad this is,' he said. 'But mates are mates.'

'Leave your wallet in the glovebox,' I said. 'Just take a bit o cash.'

I parked up on the country road, stuffed my Harrington on the backseat. Engine off. Listened.

Boom. Flutter.

15

NEVER SLEEP UNDER THE BORRACHERO TREE

MARBLE FOYER. WE mooched around. A carrot-top having a gander at the brochure stand clocked us on the way past – creased linen suit, gym bag on the floor.

'Hey there,' he went. Pearly gnashers, Desperate Dan chin.

A fucking Yank.

Gordon scoffed, wandered up to have a nosey at some footy screens on the wall.

'Work here?' I said.

'Naw.'

'We're just havin a ride out. Thought we'd try n blag our way in for a trial sesh.'

'Would you settle for a brochure?' he said, all teeth.

'Ta, mate, but our Gordon would rather go for the tour.'

In the middle of the lobby was a tree with droopy white flowers in a great glass box. I went by it, up to the fancy reception. Polished stone counter. Empty. I rang the bell a couple of times but nobody appeared.

I rang it again. Gordon shouted up the lobby: 'Bloody typical that, a posh do like this. Eff all staff about.' His eyes darted back and forth between me and the footy screens.

We sat down on some plush lounge seats in front of the reception. Tasty spread on the coffee tables: *Game Hunting Monthly. Cheshire Rifle Association. Horse & Hound.* But at least they had Gordon's number: *Total Power Lifting*, Christmas 95 edition. Well-thumbed.

The Yank was sat two chairs down from us. He picked up a *National Geographic.* 'You boys waiting on somebody?'

'You a member?' I said.

'Naw, I'm waiting on somebody who is.'

Gordon said to me: 'Oo do we know that's a member o this poncy racket?'

'Frank,' I said.

I saw Gordon's brow become an angry kiddies' Etch-A-Sketch:

Fork into a V.

Shake.

Mad squiggle.

Shake.

Back to blank.

'You on holiday over here?' I said to the Yank.

'Sorta business – pleasure.'

'What's your work, mate?'

'I'm a travel journalist and a freelance photographer. Mainly a photographer right now.'

Gordon yawned and said: 'Yer tek pictures n that?'

Toothy grin. 'Yes.'

I looked across at the tree with the white flowers. The Yank looked over too. I realised there were heat lamps in the base and its tall glass box didn't have a lid.

'What of?' I said.

'People. Places. Cities. Even trees.'

'Ever climbed a few?' I said.

'I'm sorry?'

'To take a couple on the sly. Pictures.'

'Sure,' he laughed. 'Why not.'

Our Gordon said: 'What yer doin over ere then?'

'A little corporate work. That kinda thing. They've got me staying up in Manchester.'

'What you make o that?' I said.

'The bomb?' he said.

'The tree,' I said.

He looked over again. 'I think it's striking.'

'Ow come they got it behind glass? It's a tree, not a bloody tiger,' Gordon went.

The Yank laughed. 'It's a Borrachero tree. An entheogen. They're native to Colombia, Ecuador, places like that. The flowers can be deadly. Pretty though.'

I said: 'You know a lot about trees, mate.'

Gordon said: 'Fuck me – it's a pissin plant. We goin in or what? Int there some popsy on reception we could slip a tenner to?'

The Yank flashed us his teeth again: 'I don't believe it's that kinda place.'

'It's always that kind o place. Here we go,' I said.

Hard heels tapping hard floor – echoes up the lobby. The three of us watched this young bird in a toffee-coloured office suit go behind the counter.

'Right,' said Gordon – eyes to the Yank, thumb tipped my way. 'Watch this flash fucker slap on the charm.'

I went back over.

'Hi,' she said. 'Welcome to the Florencia, or as some of our members call it, "The Playground".' Late-twenties, good skin, bottle blonde. She'd gone to town with the red lippy.

'Make you say that to everyone, do they?' I said.

'You're not a member.'

'Spose to be down for two day passes, love.'

Red smile: 'Name?' Rachel was on her name tag.

'Holland. Frank.'

'Company?'

'The Britton Bar and Restaurant Limited.'

'In Manchester? Oh – my boyfriend took me there. The food's gorgeous.'

I smiled. 'I'm a partner.' One and a half per cent. Fucking Frank.

'I can't find anything here but don't worry – Sundays have been really quiet, past few weeks.' She fussed with her fringe then opened a drawer below the counter.

'Pool opens at twelve, shuts at four. Everything else is open till six. We've the male changing rooms down the corridor to the right.' She handed me a couple of forms. 'Just fill these out first. Here's a pen.'

I waved Gordon over.

'Robbery! Fer a fuckin day pass? Fuck off!'

We made it through to the changing rooms. Gordon dropped the sports holdall on the damp tiles. Metal clunked.

I said: 'You should be doin cartwheels on the ceilin. You're still a grand up from last week, thanks to us.'

Dead Den. Burundanga.

'Well am thirty-two quid lighter now ant ah? Fuckin ell. Usually wise wiv the pennies, me. Big time.'

It was a long changing room with a strip of pale bench running round the sides, tall silver lockers above.

A few Cheshire fairies were coming and going from the showers at the bottom end. Purple flip-flops on their feet. Johnson's shampoo in their eyes.

Gordon pulled off his Henri Lloyd long-sleeve. His enormous back was blotchy skin, ugly, human granite. He twisted round – a heavy ribcage, keg-shaped, elbows by his sides, giving cleavage to his pecs. He had a bit of a roid gut going on and his shoulders had developed all sorts of bumps. The triceps had come on a few inches since the last time I'd seen him without a shirt. He took the rest of his kit off. 'What yer lookin at, puff?'

129

'You. It's Weight Watchers on a Thursday at the Rec Centre, y'know.'

I kept in good shape but I wasn't on the juice.

'Get fucked,' he said. 'Ay, oo were that Yanky twat, anyway?'

'Back there? You heard as much as I did. Don't know who he was.'

'Well ee were somebody. Smarmy cunt.'

I got changed, took the pressed blue towels out of the locker, shoved a quid in the slot and locked the sports bag inside.

'Yer sure bout all this?' Gordon said, quieter.

I shrugged. I pocketed the locker key and handed him his towel. 'Sod it. It's a day out, init?'

Gordon wanted the free-weights bar but some other lads – sandy hair, red cheeks, Macclesfield Marys – were pissing about with it. We settled for a Smith's machine. Gordon loaded the bar and let me on the bench first.

He said: 'Yer know the thing bout our Debs?'

'Go on,' I said, then: 'just a twenny for now, mate.'

Gordon took the ten off the end and left me with a twenty on either side. 'She were a talker. Not a talker, me. Not wiv birds am not. She did the talkin fer us. Easyfuckinpeasy.'

'Not a talker, he says. You could whinge for England.'

'Speakin o talkin, Frank were gettin us all mobiles nex munf.'

'I'll sort you out, don't worry. Thinkin about needin

one meself.' I took the bar off the pegs and tested the weight. I did a slow set of twelve, felt it hold my muscles – not the other way round – felt it tighten things up. 'Remember . . . Sharon?' I said, struggling with the last rep.

'Member er!? Oh-aye, yer Paki mate was onto er fer a bit wan't ee? Bloody time ago.'

I had a breather. ' . . . Maz? Yeah.'

I looked up and saw Gordon stood over me, upside down. He said: 'Sharon, fuck. Don't even go there. Might as well be on phone, bookin yerself in fer clinic while she's still suckin yer off. Jus save time. Best keep yer wick covered there, lad.'

'You remember Alice?' I said.

'Oo?'

'Alice. Alice Willows.'

'Nah. Why?'

'Before your time, then.'

'Ah. Fuckin – she what this is about, then? This Alice oo-ever?'

'You're a good lad, Gordon. Doin all this – never askin any questions.'

'Fuck it, yer right, mate. Am a saint, me. Am ere ant I? No clue why. Should be watchin cup ighlights.'

'Your go,' I said, sliding off the bench.

He took my place, flat on his back, arms up, half-glove fingers flexing, testing the bar.

'What you havin?' I said.

'Uh, we'll try sixty fer eight reps then will go from there.'

'Not forty? Two twennies?'

'Nah.'

I put them on.

'Am not avin it.'

'What?'

'Put anuva ten on each.' He bashed out a few quick reps to warm up. Too fast, showing off, doing him no good. Then he hooked the bar back up and said: 'Bout Frank . . . ah dunno. It's to do wiv the fire n all that bollocks, init? Plus the bombin – the Paddy shit las munf. What's bin goin on. Ee's keepin a bead on every cunt. Wants to know what's what. If the business is in trouble, our Frank's fucked off. Same ol story. Ee got smashed in aid o Formby las night, "God rest im," allothat. But our Frank ated is fuckin guts.'

We did a couple more sets each and then took our towels away.

There were a few birds about. Some lookers on the cross-trainers, lip-gloss and Lycra, trying their best not to break a sweat. But even Gordon didn't seem too arsed. The ponces over on the free bar were talking more than they were lifting. Their heads turned as we came over to the weight floor.

I said: 'Oi, finished ere?'

'Yes.'

But they didn't move.

Gordon said: 'Shift then. Our turn now, dick eds.'

None of them looked scared. One smiled. But they left.

Gordon took the bench.

I said: 'Calm down, lad. Don't want um makin any complaints.'

'Fuck um.'

'What you want on?'

He lay back. 'Max the fucker out.'

He bashed out some more reps – his face orange. Spit went flying – he sucked more air into his gob, his lips turned white.

My turn. He fucked off to the water fountain. I was fine for the first set but I felt the bar go on my last rep. The balance tipped. My teeth grinding, adrenaline gave me extra strength but not enough – heart rate like jungle BPM, the dull pain in my temple where Gordon had lamped me – pounding – danger.

Fuck.

Then some of the weight was cut.

A hand came down from the sky and pulled the bar up in the middle. I managed to rest it back on the pegs.

'Cheers for the spot, mate,' I said. I forced a grin – sat up, controlling my breath.

A lean body like some Soviet Olympic gymnast. Tight knots of muscle. All chest, shoulders, no waist. Dark hair, cold blue eyes, skin so pale it was almost clear, veiny. Everything about him said Balkan nutcase. He nodded and turned away, a rose-and-eagle tattoo across the back of his shoulders, poking out between the straps of a gym vest.

It was him.

I watched him go over to the Yank, who was now in red short-shorts and a *Just Do It* T-shirt. The two of them stood talking for a moment out of earshot, a daft-looking pair, then got on the treadmills.

It was him. I was sure.

The bloke from Formby's photos. The one shagging Safir and the Doll Princess. Photos signed by a Lance.

'What yer fuckin starin at now?' Gordon was next to me, waving for me to shift off the bench. We did some more upper-body work for an hour, but I kept one eye on Rose and Eagle, a cardio junkie. He worked between the rowers, cross-trainers, bikes – jumped rope like a champ on the mats. He did some stretches afterwards. The Yank gabbed in his ear all the way.

Gordon and I went over.

The Yank caught us first. 'So I see you made it in? Well done, gentlemen. Sweet talk worked out all right, huh?'

I held out my hand. 'I'm Bane. This is—'

'Gordon, right?'

Gordon nodded.

'Craig Pendergrass,' he said, looking at both of us. 'And this is . . .'

He turned to Rose and Eagle.

'. . . Emil.'

'Alright, mate,' I said.

He nodded like before. Shook my hand. Shook Gordon's.

Craig said: 'His people own a stake in The Florencia. So what is it you boys do?'

'We run a restaurant in Manchester,' I said. 'The Britton.'

'In the cenner, right?'

'Yeah. Deansgate.'

'Deansgate, right, yeah, I was there Monday. Terrible about that bomb. Your place does some great food, though. Real great food. Open late.'

Gordon butted in: 'Pricey, like, but decent specials.'

Craig laughed. 'Okay, we're heading to the bathhouse. You guys coming?'

I said: 'Gunna do a bit more first. We'll see you later.'

We watched them walk off.

Gordon said: 'What was ee called – ah meal?'

'Em il.'

'Ee got summat to do wiv yer bird?'

'Alice? Dunno, maybe. You can ask him for us.'

'We duffin im up? That tart n the Yanky cunt? That why we're ere?'

'Let's see what they do first. Best not make anyone send for the bacon wagon yet.'

There were only four people in the swimming pool, and one of them got out as we followed the signs round the side. A foreign-looking lifeguard was trying his chances with two wannabe glamour girls – plastic Pamela chests, flat arses, heavy tan. We slipped behind the pool while he was busy. The notice read:

BATHHOUSE

GOLD CARD MEMBERS

MEN ONLY

←HYBRID STEAM ROOM   **SAUNA→**

'Bit whatsit that, init? Bit sexist,' said Gordon.

I looked at him, gobsmacked.

We went in. They wanted us to stuff our kit inside square boxes of wall shelving and wear the towels. Most of the squares were still empty.

I glanced down at my joggers and Adidas. There were a couple of old blokes down to swim shorts, trotting back out to the pool area. We got some funny looks.

When the tiled corridor was clear, I went to the wall, cracked a little glass box and set off the fire alarm.

Gordon laughed over the bell. 'Mad fucker, you. Gunna send fer the bacon wagon now.'

'Come on.'

'Tell she's fussed,' Gordon said, looking up.

Further in the bathhouse – the alarm quieter, ringing back at the pool and the gym. We heard the receptionist on a tannoy speaker reading out instructions: 'Please leave all clothing and equipment . . . do not go back to your locker . . . use the fire exits located at the . . . assemble on the front car park . . .'

The air was getting muggy. One or two young lads barged past us and then more sorry-looking members of the old brigade in their purple Speedos – rich Prestbury stock. Grumbling farmers with a few bob. All kinds of well-to-do sorts wanted out, bouncing off Gordon's Conan shoulders as they met us down the corridor.

We followed Craig's voice to the steam room. Two shapes behind the thick cloud of stinging heat. Emil sat on a strip of wooden bench, a blue towel over his thighs, shorts and vest in a pile to one side. He was glazed like a seal – resting forward, head down, putting his weight on his knees.

Craig was next to him. He strained through the mist at our clothes. Smiled wide. 'Guys? Think we're supposed to—'

Emil didn't look up.

'Have him,' I said.

The towel fell as Emil stood and dragged Craig onto his feet by his neck. He drove his head back into the wall with a right hand and snapped him on the temple with a left hook. Craig keeled over to the side – head lolling like a flower on a broken stalk. Not even a second spared.

Gordon looked at me – the speed of it stopped us both. Gordon went for a grab but Emil slipped underneath, lunged forward and knocked the shit out of my solar plexus. One hit and I doubled over. Two more and I tumbled down through the fog, sinking to the tiles. Chest pounding like fuck.

Choking, I saw Emil through the heat, butting Gordon when he came in with a right swing. Keeping the distance closed, he brought an elbow down on Gordon's collarbone, forcing him to crouch. I was still clawing for oxygen. Drowning. Gordon tried a rugby tackle but Emil shoved him off balance – a quick turn, arm under the throat, and a head met the hardwood edge of the benches. The whole row shook. Gordon slumped onto his back. We were finished. I slipped in the wet, Adidas squeaking. I couldn't find my feet. Emil picked his towel back up and wiped his forehead and dropped it again. He came towards me. Stark bollock naked. Short fat cock swinging free as a bird. I saw his face – blue eyes glittering down through the vapour. He picked me up to knock me down again. One brain rattler and my eyesight went. Everything shivered. Upside down. Damaged. I could feel myself wheezing. Taste the salty scum between the floor tiles. I listened hard. Heard him slide his shorts back on, snap the waistband under his stomach. He said something. Foreign words. A question. But what did it fucking matter now? Someone else was there. I melted away.

16
CONFETTI

THE COLD SOUND – a machinery fan. A bright fluorescent stain above me ticked and hummed. I twisted onto my front, made it to my knees – fell forward again, my hands catching my weight. I breathed in. Forced my eyes to focus. Breathed out. A cable of snot and spit connected the tip of my nose to the floor, an inch or two long. A dank mesh floor. Exposed piping. Water seemed to hiss from everywhere.

I stood up and cold sweat ran down my neck. The ceiling light blinked. My pockets were empty.

Craig was on the floor, still out of it. He was wearing his short-shorts again. Emil must've dressed him when he moved us. Maybe that lifeguard helped.

The Florencia was a posh place, right out in the sticks, run by some shady foreign buggers.

The room he'd shifted us into was small – smaller

than the steam room. One door. No window. No Gordon.

The side of my head was sticky. Eye socket, caning. I had a chill. I made two fists. Relaxed. Made them again. Ignored it.

'Oi,' I said. I rocked Craig's shoulder with my foot. Nothing.

I stood on his hand and he groaned. I let him tug his hand free and he curled up like a burning leaf.

'I have a kid — I have a fucking kid . . .'

He linked his hands behind his head and started to cry.

I crouched and pulled them apart, touching his face. 'Calm it down. Look at me, mate. Calm it down.'

'Where are we?' he said.

'H-VAC. Engineer room B.12.'

'How . . .?'

'Fuckin says so.' I pointed to the plate above the door.

His red eyes strained — two cracked marbles. A front tooth was chipped. 'Is this — is this the basement?'

'Tell us everythin. Bout Emil. The shooters. The lot.'

'I don't — God, I don't understand.'

'Does the name Safir mean owt to you?'

'No.' Craig shut his eyes, welling up.

I squeezed his throat, let go when he coughed. 'Ay? Speak up, lad.'

'Yes,' he said.

'Let's have it then.'

'I can't . . .' He put his hands back over his face. Blubbering, a right state.

I said: 'Oi, mate – this feller's comin back to snuff us. If I can get us out I will. I'm the only chance you've got. Now there's no fuckin time to piss about so tell us what y'know.'

'Kay.'

'Good lad.'

He wiped his eyes, cleared his throat, started: 'Emil. He paid me to take photographs of her screwing him and some other girl at her apartment. Ten grand. Sterling. Two instalments. They wanted usable prints. Somebody who knew what they were doing. But – I didn't fucking know who she was.'

'The other bird?'

'Somebody working with Emil. Whole thing was a set-up. He didn't tell me everything. Just said it was for his associate.'

'Lance?'

'What? No, I don't know who – I mean I never met him.'

'Go on.'

'I delivered the first set of prints to Emil. Then next thing I know, I'm seeing Safir's picture everywhere. The papers here tell me she's dead. Daughter of some Egyptian millionaire? Oil money? Sweet fucking Lord, I mean—'

'Then what?'

'I kept some copies back. Put them in a safety deposit box for insurance. For protection. I was gonna mail them Stateside tomorrow morning.'

'Where they now?'

'The Great Port Hotel, on – on the street near the—'

'I know it.'

'Sorry.'

'What room?'

'222.'

'What number?'

'What?'

'For the box.'

'5-5-2-6-9. What, you gonna remember that?'

I tapped his cheek. 'Course. Now, you know anythin bout a video?'

'What video? No. I don't know anything.'

Craig wasn't fibbing. 'So, why the fuck, after what you've just said, are you here with him today?'

He was about to cry again. Soft as shite. 'Today was pay day. The other half.'

'He was gunna snuff you, mate. We just made him get round to it sooner.' I helped him off the floor.

The door wasn't locked. No time for Emil to find the engineer's key. Outside – a skinny brown corridor. Swinging doors at both ends. Another door opposite.

I tried the handle for the one in front. The room stank.

Gordon had come round. He was on his feet.

'You alright, lad?' I said.

'Me? Fuckin yeah, why?'

'You've just had the shit kicked out o you. We both have.'

'Yer dint say ee were a karate expert. A fuckin whirlwind, ee were. Yer never said owt. Chuck fuckin Norris nabs yer bird yer say fair play. Yer fuck off. That's that.'

Gordon had about five stone on Emil. His nose looked broken and his inside lip was bleeding like mad, blood coming out between his teeth as he talked – white polo shirt splattered with it.

'I don't know anythin bout anythin yet,' I said.

'Then oo the fuck is ee?' he said.

'Fuck knows. But I reckon he did Formby n his boys. The shooters belong to his lot. He torched the Kitchen Club. Mate, I know he did.'

'N then there's this feller. What's is story?'

'Craig?' I said, turning round as he shut the door behind us, red eyes wide with fear.

'Nah, this one.' Gordon twisted side-on. There was a chubby little bloke strapped to a chair behind him.

It was as if something had gnawed off the end of his nose. Rats. There were nasty chew-scabs on his face. Black bearded cheeks, black hair – tatty – all over the show. A dark heavy face, shiny with sweat, pure misery. Flab under a stretch of white shirt – soggy, yellowed.

'Abdul Muhsi,' I said.

His lips were twitching. He was drugged up – chanting something faint under his breath.

'Has he said owt?' I said.

Gordon said: 'Not a fuckin sausage. Get no sense out o this one. Ee's jus bin barkin at me in this wog speak.'

'You've a way with words, mate.'

Gordon grinned, mouth filling up with blood again. 'Ant ah jus, mate. N ee hums. Pongs. Bin ere fer fuckin time. Thev fed im n that, see?'

There was an open box of Rice Krispie knock-offs to one side, holes in the cardboard. A two-litre bottle of Virgin Cola. Open cans of food spilt across the floor. The room was the same size as the other one but with a higher ceiling. There were storage cabinets in one corner. On the other side was a great big boiler tank mounted into the wall, a poster tacked on the side with safety no-nos and pictures of unlucky stickmen. Two Calor-gas cylinders were next to the tank, upright, caged into the wall, the valves poking out the top.

I went over to Muhsi and lifted his head. Gordon had taken the gag off him. 'Iya. I'm Bane. This lad's Gordon. You just havin a kip down here, or what? You the cleaner?'

He stopped chanting.

'So now, tell us what's been goin on?'

Gordon said: 'Oi, darkie. Speak English or what?'

'Uh . . .'

'There's cleanin gear in the cupboard,' Gordon said.

'Pour summat in is eyes. Then ee'll be all go.' He went over and showed me what was on offer.

'Gordon,' I said.

Abdul moaned.

Gordon knocked over tubs of product, tutted and whistled. He pulled out a gallon tub and slid it across the floor to me with his foot. Industrial bleach.

'Not very safe storin all this in ere. Somebody's gunna get the fuckin sack. Start wiv this, mate. Work our way up. Now ee can tell us what the fuck's bin goin on.'

'Gordon,' I said. 'Just let us do it, yeah?'

'. . . I failed her,' Abdul said, 'I failed her . . .'

I let his head drop and said to Gordon: 'Probably got him on that same gear we found up in Cast Street.' Then: 'Craig?'

'Yeah?'

'You recognise this one, mate?'

'From the papers.'

'Anywhere else? He may have been shaggin a scrawny lad with blond hair? Went by Gerry.'

'Look, I swear, I don't know what you're talking about.'

'Yeah, yeah.'

Craig jumped back from the door as it opened.

Emil was showered. He wore a loose charcoal suit, dark plain T-shirt underneath. His hair was still wet. Arms straight by his side, he held the sports holdall from our locker in his left hand. The bag was unzipped.

I checked my empty pockets again.

'Bout fuckin time,' Gordon went.

One of the gas cylinders next to me had a collar on the valve but the other had been cut off. I opened it.

Hiss.

Emil lifted the bag up and then let it fall to his foot, the MP5 now in both hands.

I said: 'Fire that n we're all fuckin dead, mate. Do it. COME ON THEN!'

Emil's mouth was a line. He eyed us all, cool and steady.

Craig begged, back pressed to the far wall.

Gordon inched his way closer to Emil.

Emil dropped the machine gun and took a step back out the door. He pulled a stubby little automatic from his jacket and fired twice quickly, straight into the room, Gordon and I diving opposite ways out of the crossfire, already after the bullets had flown.

Emil walked into the room again – gun still aimed, making sure Muhsi wasn't going to be asking for the time.

Blood seeped out from Muhsi's chest – absolute black.

The gas cylinder was hissing away.

There was no boom, no fire, nothing.

Just a poor sod – a dead man – leaking royal, tied to a chair.

I was still down when Gordon managed to land one. The brick fist caught Emil on the neck, shaking him like a buoy.

'Av it.'

The shooter went. With two hands free, Emil cuffed

Gordon away and found himself some space, found a wall for his back. Gordon took a jab as he tried to rush him, we both had a go – we were all over him – Emil dodging around with prize-fighter style. Then I staggered after the little shooter – clocked Craig, useless in the corner – grabbed the gun off the floor, held it up – out – my arm straight – thumbed down the hammer.

'Gordon,' I said.

He waggled his jaw, spat, closing forward on Emil slowly. Gordon's face was bleeding, eyes dead to it all.

'Gordon!'

Emil rubbed his neck. Coughed. Blue eyes constant. 'Big marn,' he said.

Gordon went for Emil but he couldn't keep hold of him. He was too burly for the room. Emil made it look easy.

Hiss.

I had the fucking gun but I couldn't fire it.

Then Gordon threw him against the boiler tank. The drum rang, echoing through the pipes as he bounced onto the floor, clumsy for the first time. Gordon spat on him. 'Cunt.'

Emil rested his back up against the tank. His face still, legs stretched out, like he was mending already. He wiped the bloody goz off his head with his forearm and looked up at his gun in my fist.

'Let's have it then,' I said. 'Before you go.'

He put his hand inside his trouser pocket and dug out a fat gold lighter. Flicked open the lid and held it up high, near the open valve.

Craig whimpered.

Gordon laughed.

I squatted down, pressed the nose of the gun into Emil's forehead. His eyes closed. Harder. Like it would break through his skull. His thumb was flat – pushing the lighter wheel, about to spark the flame.

'Come on,' I said. 'Let's do one. Our Craig's not cut out for this.'

We left Emil and made a break for it. Didn't look back. Craig was first out, Gordon last – probably wishing he could've put the boot in one more time. Craig chose left through the corridor, bounced through the swinging door, panting.

I saw him stop ahead of me, heard music playing inside the next room. We all froze when we got there. A square room with ventilation fans and double doors at the far end, but no windows – we were underground.

There was a stereo blaring out some naff Abba tape. Two lines of workbenches and a kitchenette unit, coke presses, a microwave, a shooter on the table, heat lamps, plant clippings stacked up, white droopy flowers, mortar and pestle, piles of gear – all sorts – uncut, cut, bricked-up, ready to shift.

Five stools. Five pasty foreigners.

They stopped what they were doing – looked at us. Masks under their chins, blue latex gloves hovering over scales, tubs of lidocaine. Dead to rights.

The feller nearest said something at us in his own language. Nobody said anything. He barked it again, angry. He pointed at me. To the gun still in my hand. I held it flat side in my palm. *CZ 99*.

Nobody knew what to do next. I wrapped my fingers around the handle and aimed it out as a warning. 'Oi.' He was going for the shooter on the table. He backed off, hands up, jabbering, jabbering as the three of us came further into the room.

The music drowned him out.

'The Winner Takes It All'.

Noise burst into the room from behind us. Deafening. Craig fell on me, trapping me down under a workbench.

The noise ripped the place up, swallowed Abba, spat out flower petals and gore like confetti, clouds of coke and burunfuckingdanga. Shit knows what else.

Shoot. Kill. Everything.

Emil mowed the workers down, chewed them all, his finger never off the MP5 trigger.

I clocked our Gordon ducking on the other side of the room. He'd taken a couple in the arm. Maybe more. He was a big target.

I shrugged Craig off me. He was pulsing with blood.

I fired at Emil. The noise stopped. He dropped back out the door.

We scarpered.

Gordon was a mess.

'Fuckin bastard . . . fuckin bastard . . . what a fuckin day, ay?'

I wasted another bullet behind me to give us a bit of time but did my wrist with the recoil.

The window inside a locked wooden door showed us a stairwell. A bullet later and we were up three flights and out the door at the top. The bathhouse service entrance was locked to the left of us. A fire exit opposite. Gordon sagged his weight across the bar – triggering the fire alarm again as the door opened.

Daylight.

The Florencia rear car park. I saw the swimming pool through the glass across the back end of the building.

We weaved through the parked cars, kept low – Gordon's arm over my shoulder, he was doing his best.

'Good God,' a toff went, creaking out of a Range Rover in front of us.

'Should see uva feller,' Gordon said.

The toff's gob fell open, showing off his big false gnashers. He squeezed back against the 4x4 to let us pass.

Gordon said: 'What yer lookin at, mate? That's right – trap shut. Trap shut.' He snatched at my wrist, his grip still strong, and waved my gun hand up in the air, smiling.

'Gordon,' I said.

'Fuck um.'

Car park ended. I dragged him through a gap in the hedges and into a field. Into the cow shit, barbed weeds, thickets, woods ahead. We grafted our way out of the undergrowth. The sticks started here.

I sat Gordon down against a fat tree, took my black polo off, scrunched out the blood and wiped my face, turned it inside out and put it back on. I spewed. He said: 'Don't mind us.'

'Keep that arm above your head,' I said.

I left him to fetch the chariot.

17

ME DAD PART 2

'WATCH ME BAD shoulder.'

'Oo's this knob ed?' Gordon went.

'Your old man,' I said. 'Dozy bugger.'

'Alright, Dad. Seen me polo? State of it. Only ad it on five minutes. Bloody ruined. Want refund.'

Vic said: 'If ee ad a fez ee'd be Tommy Cooper.'

It was a job to, but with one end each, we managed to lift Gordon from the car into Vic's taxi. We propped his arm on the back headrests, above his heart. A rag to cover the whole mess from any keen Sunday drivers eyeing the back window when Vic got him on the road.

'Comfy, mate?' I said.

'Pillow would be grand.'

'Grapes?'

'Bane, av not ad . . . this much ova laugh since . . .

since that bargain-boozer wareouse . . . raid . . . fun in them freights.' He was bobbing in and out.

Vic said: 'Pipe down, piss ed.' He kicked Gordon's shoe, sticking out the door.

Gordon smiled through a wince, tipped his head back onto the inside glass. He was so white he was blue.

Vic said to me: 'What's ee ad?'

'Finished off a bottle o gin in the car,' I said.

'Ow much of it went down is gob n ow much went on is arm?'

'Gob in first place won gold. Arm didn't even get a medal.'

'That's me boy. Mard as a bloody fairy.'

'He's had us in stitches,' I said.

'Ee'll need more than bloody stitches.'

No bullets to extract. Two exit wounds, strips of chicken dangling off the bone. We'd taken the shirt tourniquet off and then strapped him up before moving him. We'd eaten through a heavy tin of first aid from the boot. Iodine and bandage tape and gauze and even lidocaine. Some of it fairly fucking useless. All of it better than nothing. Vic liked to think he could get hold of anything. Druggy or doctor, if it got left in his cab it was his. And his to keep or sell.

We were seven miles away from The Florencia. A dirt track off the nearest B-road by a broken kissing gate. Rusty tractor skeleton down the lane, missing three tyres. A red phonebox at the top end. Paint peeling. Mud-flaked windows. 'Tiff the Randy Rambler' had stuck her calling card inside.

Good job taxi drivers aren't bad with directions. Another ten minutes and his son would've been dead.

'Ow ard was ee, mate?' Gordon said.

I ducked my head into the taxi.

'Hard.'

Gordon grinned: 'Soz ard, mate . . . Ee were . . . fuckin soz ard.'

'No shame when they're soz hard, is there, Vic?' I said, looking back out at his dad.

'No shame, son. No shame.' He pushed Gordon's feet into the taxi and closed the door on him. I looked in through the glass – Gordon's eyes shut. Out cold.

Vic came round to the boot and took his daft trilby off. He put it up on the blue flat of the roof. The tears came down. He wiped them out with the heel of his hand. 'Fuck me. Ee's a right do. Enry, what the fuck, lad? Ay?'

I put my hand on his good shoulder. Useless weight.

'Soz ard?' he said. 'Me boy's bin shot. Our lad. Shot. Not some fuckin scrap at footy stand.'

'He's bin shot before, Vic.'

'Used to it be now should ah? Ay!?'

'Vic—'

'Ee can't fuckin go ospital. Not our Gordon. Not like this wiv is record. But ee's gunna lose that arm anyway. That's me fuckin boy. The daft dozy blinkin ooligan. N now it's all over.' Vic sobbed.

'What you gunna do?' I said.

'Ah dunno. Al tek im somewhere. Ah will. Ah know where ah cun go get im fixed up maybe. Doctor what owes us a favour.' He tugged his gaping Crombie sleeves up to his elbows. Bony wrists. Silver fuzz on each arm. Hands in pockets in search of fags. Yellow claws snatched one out of the box, dropped it on the way to his mouth, dropped the pack after it.

'Shit.'

'Dry your eyes, Vic. He'll be right.' I crouched and fished them out the mud.

He nodded, put a hand round the back of my neck, reeled me in for a hug.

Back to the car – blood-soaked upholstery in the mirror. Eyes higher: a taxi indicating at the top of the lane. I wound the window down. It was muggy inside and out.

I knifed the ignition. Twist. The dash clock lit up. Not even 2 p.m. Twist. Neneh Cherry cried through the radio. Twist. The engine cried with her.

18

THE DOG IN 222

ANCOATS. THE FLAT. Front door on the Yale since the shoot bolt was broken. *Gordon.* I caught a splinter on the frame inspecting the damage second time round. At least it would shut.

I checked I was alone. Showered. Aching. Checked everything was where I'd left it – two bags, one brick – shooters still out of sight. No time to move them. Here was as safe as anywhere.

Maybe the guns belonged in the basement of that health club. Emil's lot could've shifted them to Otterburn Close after Friday night's sweet hat-trick. Somewhere closer to hand. If there was truth in that, then they would've seen more action soon.

I filled my wallet with more of Den's cash and hid Emil's little shooter. I stopped on my way out, went back in again, put the gun in my Harrington and left.

'No money. Do not want money.'

'It's fifty bloody quid,' I said under my breath.

'Do not want money.' She squeaked the room-service trolley to the next door but I pushed it into an alcove in the hallway.

'No!' She spun round, frantic.

A stack of clean towels on the bottom shelf tipped onto the carpet. I stamped the wheel brake on against a cold radiator and loads of dirty cups and saucers wobbled on the top tray.

I said: 'Take it. Fifty quid. You mithered bout gettin the sack? Even if you did—' I pulled my wallet back out, gave her a dog-eared compliment card for the Britton. She took it. No nail varnish. She read it blank-faced, over and over, eyes on a loop. 'The Britton,' I said. 'Waitressin. Frank's always after staff. He'll bollock you every now n then but he'll pay you more than this lot do.'

'More?' She looked up – gob open, gormless. Good teeth. She was anywhere between fifteen and thirty. Dark-dark bob, chipmunk cheeks, no make-up. An illegal.

'Just not much more,' I said.

'Britton.' She looked at the card again – held it in both hands. She dithered, fell back a few inches, rested her little shoulders flat against the vintage wallpaper – swallows and red beanstalks – the pattern like a nosebleed.

'Don't be daft,' I said.

She flicked the card into the tea dregs on the top of the trolley and crouched to collect the spill of towels. There was a rosary round her neck. She was a decent cup size. 'Please. Go. Do not want money. *Please.*'

Some bird popped out of a room at the bottom of the hall and shouted down: 'Oh – while yer ere, love, can we grab n extra towel?'

The maid stood up and fetched one over to her.

The key cards were stacked in an empty ice-cream tub on the back end of the trolley. I flapped through the lot while she was gone, wagging my index, making them clap together – blur.

222.

I slotted the fifty between 221 and 223 as a placeholder.

I heard the door shut down the bottom end. The maid shot back up the corridor.

'No. Please. No.'

I held the key up out of reach. 'Keep your voice down, love.'

She leapt for it, short nails dug in my forearms like she wanted to climb me.

'I'm tryin to help you, love.'

'Go fuck off.' She went to slap me and caught my ear instead.

The key card swapped hands behind my back. Quick eyes – no colour – they didn't miss a trick.

She jumped for it again, caught a foot on the trolley wheel and tripped forward. I tried to catch her but she fought my hands away. Her knees met the floor. The saucers on the trolley rattled for ages.

'The Britton,' she spat. 'Food for dogs.'

'Nah. Grub's better than that.'

'Look at your face. Your face. Never trust a dog.'

'It's a bruise, love. Settle down.'

'No. No.'

She pulled the trolley leg to help her get on her feet faster. The trolley tipped. Dirty crockery smashed. A right din. Fucking soap bars and towels and toilet rolls flopped on the carpet – this sliding heap.

I watched her on the floor, scooping things up with her uniform, making it clatter more. She gave up. Sat back on her legs. *'Jak sobie pościelesz, tak się wyśpisz,'* she said, looking up at me.

You reap what you sow.

'Nie ma tego złego co by na dobre nie wyszło.' I said, walking away.

Every cloud has a silver lining.

I'd picked up one or two turns from Frank's chefs. Those being the one or two.

The view from Craig Pendergrass's room stretched over London Road. I could see grubby brick arches caked in fly-posters for the Apollo. Suits and totty with their wheelie suitcases, heading for the taxi rank. A few swanky ancient flats down the far end.

There was a camera tripod by the window but no camera. A list of smut titles on offer above the telly. Stacks of newspapers and local freebies, a Gideon Bible

159

by the bed – hardback, one of the pages thumbed down to keep his place. Odd bugger.

The safety deposit box was on the shelving underneath the coat rack.

A sticky calculator pad on the front.

5-5-2-6-9.

I pulled out an A2 envelope – Post-it stuck on the front: *Sunday 7 July 02:31 a.m.*

Not Wednesday, early hours. Not the night Safir and my Alice died.

Inside, everything Formby had been given was here, plus more. But still, nothing of Alice. There were a few clearer ones of Emil doing the business. *Emil.* Why hadn't he snuffed us there and then in the steam room? Why shift us? Was he waiting on orders from this Lance? I guess we'd tied his fucking hands by the end of it.

There were a few nasty close-ups – motion-blurred, grainy with the distance. Safir on the double bed, the Doll Princess an extra wheel. Safir touching her up the most, pulling her hair, biting her tits. I stopped on the last picture, one I hadn't seen – smudged faces, ghost lines. Safir was grinning. I came back to the start.

I took a black-and-white print and went over to the window and held it out – winked slowly, one eye open and then the other – trying to find Safir's building. Which flat. Which window. No chance – fucking impossible to tell. I dropped the photo. It surfed onto the bedspread behind me.

Craig's fancy camera gear was in a case under the bed. I opened it up on top. Everything was in bits, housed in dozens of cut-out pockets. I would've pinched this at one time just to sell it on. Now I figured it might be worth keeping. I had a play with the camera, fixed it to the biggest lens and held it up – the viewfinder was blurrier than a kid's toy. Fiddly gadgets. I twisted the lens – trial and error, clocked the windowsill by luck – tall, blocky rectangles on the side of the building. I glanced down at the photo on the bed to make sure – the only one with a snatch of the outside of the flat left in the frame.

Through the camera: I couldn't see any double beds inside the windows. The zoom was good enough but I wasn't going to have any luck during the day with the lights off. Four windows had blinds down, anyroad. But at least now I knew the building.

I took the camera apart, matched the bits back to the pockets, packed up the snaps in the envelope and shut everything in the case, good to go.

No sign of the maid when I came out. Her trolley was upright, still there. A bloke was mooching around the corridor by the lift, and the bulb above his head had gone, keeping him in shadow. Not old, not young – Joe Bloggs garb, too dark to make out his face. I nodded and walked the opposite way to the stairwell.

6 p.m. Sun still roasting. I left the chariot where it was, in the Star and Garter car park, and went by foot. A

not-so-quick stroll down the road – it all looked nearer through a camera lens.

I strutted alongside the blokes in fake Lacoste, the birds with crop-top flab, shopping bags, sunburn – heading back from Market Street. Me: twitchy, the camera-case handle greasy in my fingers. I was watching my back after every step, in broad daylight. Like skunk paranoia. Like a born victim. At least the heat was helping with the muscle aches from my run-in with Emil.

I turned right on the corner and there it was: Safir's swanky old digs. I squinted up at the tall windows, a hand over my eyes to block the sun.

There was a van between two parked Mazdas in front of the entrance. Not the same Transit but I felt it in my stomach, all the same.

I crossed over, nearly walked in front of a tram – sat on a bench near the concrete steps up to the foyer.

A podgy feller was sat on the other end, opening a choc-ice wrapper.

I turned my head and watched a couple of orange stick insects exit the door to Safir's building. The return of Ray-Bans and chiffon skirts. Spaghetti-strap tanks, open blouses. One of them turned right and walked up the pavement past the bench.

'Legs,' Choc-Ice said to me.

'Ay?'

'Jus teks a bit o sun n they all pop out the woodwork. I'm a leg man, meself.'

'We talkin chicken?' I said.

'Course. What yer partial to most?'

Breast.

'Thigh,' I said.

'Bit fatty,' he said, ice-cream in his tash. 'Dunt suit me diet.' He was ganneting it down – blue wrapper and all, it looked like.

Another shifty feller, like the one in the hotel corridor, appeared on the steps. Good posture, too obvious for dibble, but it'd make sense to have a plain-clothes bobby on guard. Our eyes met for a second. We squared – both wondering which of us looked the most trouble. I stood up, stepped out into the road and hopped on a tram, got off again around Minshull Street and then made my way back to the car – still sweating, and it wasn't the sun.

19

BAD ELVIS

LATE EVENING, STILL light. Back to the old house. I put the key in the front door and turned it, opened the door an inch and shut it again. I went round the back.

The passage stank of bins – back plots one and the same. Everyone along the row had washing out – crusty linen, flesh-coloured tights, giant pancake bras. There was a Union Jack beach towel over next-door-but-one's line, half-hidden by the weeds. Their Rottweiler pup barked at me between the gaps in the fence – teeth between every five pickets until my ankle was out of sight. I heard somebody yell out of the kitchen window: 'Trudy! Get in!'

87. I hopped over my back gate. The backdoor was a mess – lock gone – the wooden panel was a flimsy piece of tat anyway. This wasn't a PVC neighbourhood.

I pressed my side up against the door – gave it a firm, quiet shoulder and let myself in.

The door wiped away a fallen kitchen chair that had been keeping it shut. I picked the chair up and slid it back under the table.

They'd plundered my cosy kitchen – filled the sink with smashed bottles of bargain booze – empty lager cans on the worktop that they'd brought along for the fuck of it. Cupboards opened, emptied. There was nothing in my fridge, anyway. Most of the lads were always in a state after a few. At least Gordon could hold his drink.

They'd ripped a Biggie poster off the wall in the hallway. Cruel. They'd taken both mirrors down and put the glass through. Daft. They'd torn out pages from the phonebook under the stairs and paper-aeroplaned them about the place. Nice touch.

There was one message on the answerphone:

BEEP. 'Bane, lovey – it's only Jan. Jus thought ad let yer know bout funeral n that. Alice's mam rang us n she's sortin out what's what. Gunna be nex Friday mornin, she says. At eleven. Manchester Crem. Dead soon that, init? Anyway – ope yer good, lovey . . . well, al see yer there won't ah? Give us a ring if yer can. Enry? Um, ta-ra.'

I went in the front room as Jan's message finished. At least they'd saved the telly. My box of videos was out. I rifled through, found a smudged biro scrawl written on the back of a chippy menu – great big shaky letters:

WELL WELL! DID NOT NO U STILL
HAD ME FUCKIN BOXING VIDS MATE.
NOW WHERE FUCK R U?

I'd been meaning to give them back to our Gordon for three months.

I had a sit-down, the chippy menu in hand. There were fags burnt out on the arm of my new settee. Ash stamped in the rug. I'd tried to forget he'd mentioned all this when he'd clouted me back at the safe flat this morning. He was just doing his job, Gordon. It wasn't like I could be mad, especially after today.

Frank's crew. I wasn't one of the lads anymore – that was the trouble.

I wondered where Gordon was – where Vic had taken him. I'd have to send the brute his getwellsoon. If he pulled through.

The phone rang. I walked over and let it ring, ring, and click onto answerphone.

BEEP. 'Bane, the lads are tellin us you're not ome. They can't find yer at any o me flats either – least that's what they're stickin to . . .' He breathed down the line. I put my hand on the receiver but didn't pick up.

'Pick up, Bane. Pick the fuck up if you're in – now, there's a good lad, or al pour a tank o petrol down your throat before ah cut it. N al swear to that on Missus olland's—'

'Alright, Frank,' I said – receiver to ear.

'Bane.'

'Just off out. What's on?'

'Off out or off out out?'

'Neither.'

'Off out for good?'

'Looks like it.'

'Well, then. Ta-ra. Ad a better offer av we? Oo is it, by chance? Now, ah know it can't be Formby. Ee's way o the fuckin dodos. N is lot. N is club. Poor cunt.'

'Believe so, yeah.'

'Pigs say it were a shootin. One o those, what do they call it, now? *Gangland executions*. Fire was to cover their arses.'

'That right?'

'Brings a bit o heat on our place, dunt it?'

'Not for me to say,' I said.

'Bad Elvis,' he said.

'What?'

'Bad fuckin Elvis.'

'You've lost us, Frank.'

'The King? Yer think ah dint twig? Shunt talk about shit yer don't know about, Bane. Thought yer knew better than that, lad. Yuv bin workin fer us fer – what – two years? Av done yer big favours since then. Put a tidy bit o paper in your wallet. Not asked fer much. Jus the usual. Some respect.'

'Three.'

'Three what?'

'Three years.'

'Pardon me, three years. Three years n av set you n

the big lad up nicely. Speakin o the big lad, where is the fuckin gorilla? As ee gone walkies wiv yer?'

'Not heard from Gordon,' I said.

'Anyway, yuv ad it cushdy. Always ad yer on a longer leash, dint ah, Bane? Yuv more brains then the rest o that lot put together. But yer know it. Fuckin gala-vantin around now like yer run the show. Still av to maintain a bit o respect. So now yuv taken the piss wiv a disappearin act. That can urt people's feelins, that can. Pity.'

'I don't know what to say, Frank.'

'Do yer want a job? One o them proper ones? A real fuckin nine-to-five? Do yer wanna av to live like rest of um – dirty little cooped-up rats runnin bout the place till they drop dead from boredom? Get fucked. Wise up, lad.'

I said: 'You're takin this all a bit personal, don't you think?'

'Yuv come along way since ah found yer at the footy stand. Thanks to us.'

'I know.'

'But now yer think you're different from the scum-bags? That's it, init? Always was, maybe. The top man. Above the bollocks. Aren't we?'

'Gotta run, Frank. All the best.'

'Run little rat. You're not top man. Yer nowt. You're the fuckin worst of um, Bane. N if yer think you're grassin, you're in fer a fuckin shock.'

That's what this was about. 'I'm no grass,' I said. I looked down at Gordon's note.

'All the best, Bane. Jus know – al find yer soon enough. Ta-ra.'

I put the phone down. I changed my clothes. I headed out for some scran.

20

CAGNEY N CHIPS (FOR THE LONG DRIVE)

FISH AND CHIPS for tea. Why not? Go mad. The English chippy on the corner was shut on a Sunday but the Chinese was open till late. I ordered a bag of chips and some fried seafood nightmare I was already regretting by the time the bloke had handed me my change. He was a young Chinese feller. Shaved head, strong jaw, ink spokes crawling up from under his uniform collar – Celtic, not Triad.

There was a Goodmans portable telly on the counter. Cagney was on, stiff-legged, jigging in front of a backdrop. Tall, curvy birds in stripes and feathers by his side – dancing for him. It wasn't my kind of Cagney picture. I was more about Little Tough Jimmy, the grapefruit chucker. The hardcase. One of my old man's favourites.

I said: 'Lot o musicals on the box these days. Nothin else ever on.' Broadway Cagney seemed to give up. He put his hands on his hips and tried out some notes, eye candy still grafting away hard.

'ITVmusicalweekendsee.' The Chinese feller said it to me in one go, at about Mach 3.

'Ah, right.'

'Hereyougo.' He passed me my grub in a hot plastic bag after chucking in a lolly-stick fork and a menu.

'Cheers, mate.'

Past ten, dark out. I left the Chinese with my tea and crossed the road. There were still plenty of kids knocking about – a gang of them outside the off-licence, probably back from a game of five-a-side in the park. One lad was doing keepy-uppy with the ball.

'Mr Bane.'

I stopped walking.

Posh. Maybe a Southerner. Pushing forty. Wide-wide shoulders. Six-four, easy. Two inches shorter than our Gordon, and four taller than me. Brown shirt, open at the neck. Brown mac, no belt.

'Who's askin?' I said.

'Step this way, please.' There was a big gap between his top lip and bugle, crying out for a Magnum tash.

I asked him who he was.

He put an elbow in my belly, right there on the pavement, by the main road. I tipped forward in shock and my lungs emptied. His hand on the back of my neck – dragging me off the street, down between Ladbrokes and Edna's Caff.

'Step this way,' he said again.

We went along the accessway – cramped employee car park at the bottom end.

'Watch me fuckin tea,' I said, spitting on the gravel.

He locked my arms behind my back and gave me a tap in the kidneys. My knees nearly went. This wasn't my day.

He took us further down the alley. I dropped down and snatched my wrist out of his hold – lamped his jaw with my free hand as I came up again, butting him with the same momentum before I got some distance between us.

He wiped his nose and gob with the back of his fingers. 'Stupid bastard,' he went. A spring cosh shot out of his hand. He clack-clacked the gravel with the metal end like it was a white stick, blocking my way out. His nose started to bleed.

I did one down the accessway. Made for the car park, thinking I could still scale a fence quicker than this big fucker. I could hear him after me – stiff, flat-footed, not too light on his feet. Cagney's dance teacher.

I skidded to a halt in the mouth of the alley.

Wheel spin on the gravel. Angry squeal. Brakelights blinding in the dark.

The back of a white van rocked in front of me – feet thumping inside. The hinge doors opened. Grabby hands sucked me in.

'In we come, laddie.' A bloke's voice.

The Southerner's shoe up my arse, making sure. 'Fuck!'

I dropped flat onto the metal floor of the van – darkness – shooting pains in my elbows and knees. Somehow I was still holding onto my takeaway.

'Ivey,' the voice said. 'That were a bit offside, wan't it?'

I could just about see a pair of chunky boots, stood slightly apart, a few inches away. Steel toecaps.

'What happened to yer?'

'He got frisky,' the Southerner went, still behind me.

'Always smooth in the field, ay, Ivey? Pinch your nose. There's Kleenex in the glovebox. Now put your cock away n shut the doors. This one's got places to be.'

'He needs a good hiding.'

'It's a Transit not bloody KITT. Chop chop.'

The doors shut.

Real darkness.

Then light – a mucky fluorescent work light duct-taped to the inside roof of the van. There was plenty of headroom, though I wasn't quite standing up yet. I stayed low down and saw the locked compartment that led to the front. A customised vehicle.

I heard Ivey getting in the driver's seat – even in this tank, I felt the suspension dip.

'D'yer know what's what?' Forty-odd. Podgy. Tash.

I said: 'No.'

'Want us to tell yer, then?'

'Can do.'

The engine turned over. Exhaust rattled. The radio came on in the front and we were off.

'Now, oo am I?' he said. 'Tek your time.'

'Choc-Ice.'

'That's the ticket. Now, it's Bane, yeah? That's what they call yer, don't they?'

'Yeah.'

'Dougie Glassbrook.'

'That's your real name, is it?'

'Is for now.'

'So what are you, dibble?'

'Close. Try again. Up the food chain.'

'Special Branch.'

'Close enough.' He stepped forward. I could see the cuffs winking on his belt.

'I've never been inside,' I said.

'They nicked yer once or twice, though. Juvie reprimand. They don't always make the shredder, let me fuckin tell yer.'

'Get on with it.'

Steel toecap found stomach. I coiled up.

He said: 'Jus for Ivey's conk, that were. Anyroad, start us off, Bane. See, I'm gettin on a bit. Summat about *rights*?' He crouched down, breathed on my face. 'Right to remain what? Sorry, it's not come back to us yet. Carry on, laddie.'

I didn't say a word. Glassbrook stood up – booted me again in the same place – not quite as hard – but nearly fell on me as we sped round a corner. Then he put hands under my arms and propped me up, set me down on a bench seat. He grabbed the sliding bag of chips off the van floor and chucked it in my lap.

'Not a mark.' Glassbrook brushed my shoulder with the flat of his hand.

'Time for the cuffs yet?' I said.

'Hard to eat in cuffs.' He gave my shoulder a last slap and then sat on the opposite bench. 'You've paid for um. Might as well eat your tea. Be a while yet.'

'Cop shop?'

He ignored me. I unwrapped the bag of chips with one hand, the other, holding my side.

'You offerin?' he said, before I'd even got through the grease paper.

I coughed. 'Help yourself.'

He took the biggest chip – looked up to eat it like a chick being fed a worm. He scoffed it down. 'No salt on um.'

I said: 'How long you been after us?'

'Yer make it sound like I was after a kiss.'

'It's the tash.'

He took a wedding band out of his pant pocket – fiddled it down his ring finger. He made sure I saw it.

'We've bin keepin tabs on enry Bane since before he started spendin afternoons outside the deceased's flat.'

'The deceased?'

'Saafiya Hassan.'

'All a bit cloak n dagger, init?'

'Our fair city was blitzed by the Paddys jus last munf,

Bane. There's a mobile death squad on the loose, workin weekends. Think Joe soddin Public gives a flyin fuck ow we catch um?'

'I don't even wear green.'

'Canna pinch another?' he said.

I held the bag over to him, but not close enough. 'I think Manny's the last place they'll fuckin be, don't you?' I said. 'N so right now, you lot do as you please, that it?'

'Don't talk daft.' He tilted forward – arse hovering over his bench, greasy mitts out for the chips.

I pushed the bag in Glassbrook's face, stood and tackled him forward. When his head clanged the wall of the van, I let the chips drop and chinned him with a tight hook. His head flicked away – mouth exploding in teeth. His jaw was slack. A lucky strike.

He dropped down on all fours, scrambling after a tooth.

'Glassbrook?' Ivey's voice – up in the front.

My hand was caning, the wrist still not right from the pistol recoil that morning. I wrung it out, flexed the digits.

I stood over Glassbrook and said quietly: 'Don't worry, you'll be covered. Dental insurance premiums? You pigs'll have it sorted.'

Every time the revs dropped you could hear teeth bouncing around on the metal.

I stamped my foot. A gnasher lodged in the tread of my sole.

'Everything alright back there?! Glassbrook?!' We

heard Ivey yell again. The van slowed. He turned the radio down.

Crouching: 'Tell him we're sound.' I spoke with my jaw so tight it felt like my own teeth would crack. 'Tell him you fat fuckin bastard or I'll knock the rest out.'

'. . . Peachy! Everythin's peachy, Ivey! We're alright. I were jus readin him his rights n he fell over. A few times.'

'Too right he did,' Ivey called back, laughing.

We moved off again. Music on. Ivey went up the gears.

I scrubbed Glassbrook's hair for a second with the knuckles of my good hand. 'Not a bad shout.'

'Listen—' he said, his face dripping with bright hot grease, dobs of it in his eyelashes. His mouth was a mess.

'These killins have got nowt to do with the IRA,' I said.

'We know that,' he said.

'What else you know? Keep it down.' I pushed his face harder into the floor. 'Start with me.'

'We spotted yer back in Wythenshawe this mornin. Fartin about in that atchback with new plates.'

So our Maz had lent me a nicked courtesy car. I wondered if he knew about it. Probably would have got away with it any other weekend.

'Then what?' I said.

'We followed yer down the A523 to that posh keep-fit club.'

'N what happened – what went on?'

'There were jus a fire drill. Few pillocks came out. Went back in. Then the alarm went off again. We lost yer for a bit. Dint see yer come out in the end. Ad to radio in for your motor. A Panda flagged your reg in town this afternoon. We tracked yer back ere. Picked you up.' Glassbrook tried for his feet but belly-flopped back on the floor.

I took the cuffs off his belt. 'Are you mad? So you're, what – parked up outside The Florencia, right? Operation Command. Surveillance R Us. N you didn't manage to clock any o the warzone? Like the Wild West back there for a while. So how is it you missed that, Glassbrook? Five Live too loud?'

I crossed his wrists behind him.

'Are yer makin this shite up?' he said.

'Are you?'

Cuffs on. I felt mighty.

'Bane, you're messin with your life, ere, laddie. Don't be a fuckin pillock.'

'Gob shut,' I said. 'You're tellin us you two are from Special Branch? You're like somethin off the fuckin "Fast Show".' I twisted his arm until his face screwed up in pain. He started to make a fuss.

'Ivey's MoD,' he said. He almost cried out, stopped himself.

'Bite your lip, Glassbrook, sssshhh . . . there's a good man.'

'I said he's—'

'I heard. Em Oh Dee? What's that then? Ministry o Defence? Course, he is.' I rattled his cuffed hands.

'Think you're tellin us porkies, Glassbrook. Why were you after us to begin with?'

'Yer know Terence Formby, don't yer? Dead club owner – Deansgate?'

'Course. Through the trade.'

'Yer knew im well – think yer might've witnessed im go.'

'Bollocks.'

'Formby's club. Survivin staff got interviewed after the fire. Anythin out the ordinary that night. Anybody oo come in, never come out – wasn't accounted for. Anybody oo went in through the back. Like you did.'

Doorman Jamie had been chin-wagging. I said: 'Pigs could o nabbed us sooner.'

Glassbrook: 'Forget local plod. Once your record got faxed over we told um to forget yer. *We* keep the tabs.'

They'd only been following me a day.

Doorman Jamie, unaware he was in league with the fucking MoD. I nearly laughed.

'Safir,' I said. 'Thought you were investigatin who did Safir?'

'We are but—'

'Quietly.'

Quieter: 'But officially it's a separate inquiry. Death Squad n Safir. Local boys are cooperatin under Need to Know. The Supers aside, they know nuffin bout the additional investigation.'

'So tell us what you're keepin out the papers.'

'Daddy Hassan's reps in Maadi, Cairo, contacted our government yesterday. Requestin we find this Abdul

Muhsi faster. Bit of international cooperation. It's in our nation's interests that the bastard gets found.'

'Bloody hell, hope you're not in charge o the war.' I sat on the bench – Glassbrook's collar in my fist – hauled his top half upright – head resting on the wall, hands trapped behind him.

He kept sliding sideways as the van braked. I left his neck and got hold of his elbow to keep him upright. His mouth bled and bled.

'Abdul Muhsi's pushin daisies,' I said. 'Tied up, shot up. A dead hostage. Found him in the storeroom on the bottom floor o The Florencia. You n that big Lundon fairy behind the wheel are gunna do yourselves some harm.'

Glassbrook's mouth made an O. He was like a trout with a moustache.

'You know fuck all,' I said.

'We can salvage this royal cock-up,' he went.

'What can you tell us about some hardcase called Emil? Eastern European. You know who I'm on about?'

He nodded, tash dripping grease. 'You mean Emil Nikolin.'

'Well?'

He took a deep breath: 'International rep, ee has. Serbian paramilitary. Professional nutty bastard. There's rumours bout foreign protection, legit currency comin in from bugger knows where. Whitehall keep a file. Arkan's Tigers mean owt to you? Yugoslav wars?'

'Serb Volunteer Guard.'

He tried to cough quietly. 'You did read a newspaper once, dint yer?'

I smiled. 'I give um a go now n again.'

'Ee's bin over here with a Lance Mora. Doin no one's sure what – but it's involvin guns. We reckon Nikolin ad Formby n is lot stamped out. Gotta be drugs, these days.'

'Safir was involved?'

'You tell us, laddie. You're the one in the know.'

'What makes you think it was this lot?'

'Frank olland's not big enough. Chinkies aren't daft enough. Local scrappers avn't got the arsenal. Nikolin's ere. We've traced some o the burnt munitions recovered from the scene. Bags full, they were. It's Nikolin. We find the shooters n we're away.'

I stopped Glassbrook sliding as we went round a bend.

'You don't even know why I'm mithered,' I said.

'Yer knew Safir?'

'Why would someone like me know someone like her? I've just heard the rumours.'

'Then what?' he said. 'What do yer fuckin want?'

Alice.

I let him fall sideways as Ivey braked. 'You want somethin big on this Lance n Emil. I'm a rum lad with a bit o local clout. You're thinkin I can help you slap all this together with Safir, grill till golden.' I pulled him back up. 'Where you takin us?'

'Droppin yer off at the discotheque,' he said.

'On a Sunday night? I could have work tomorrow.'

'Industry night,' Glassbrook said. 'Yer should know that. This one's a private do.'

'Is there anyone followin?'

'No. Told yer. Nobody ere knows bout this. Report's not due till nex munf.'

'Gobsmacked you can write your own name.'

'We can protect you,' he went.

'Even if you could, why would you now?'

'There's a mobile in me jacket pocket. Tek it. We can contact yer tomorrow. Start this over. Get it done proper.'

'Can't help you, mate. Sorry,' I said.

'You're a smart bugger. If what you've said bout Muhsi is gospel. If we get a body. We can tek um to the cleaners.'

'Thought you were takin me?'

'We got off on the wrong foot.'

'Yeah, your foot.'

'Just tek the phone. I'm not jus tryna save me arse.'

I fished a hand into his jacket – pulled out a grey Nokia. The screen was leaking behind the glass like a broken school calculator. I opened my Harrington, put the mobile in the inside pocket – zipped it up again.

I said: 'So why am I goin dancin?'

The van stopped.

'We here?' I said.

'Yeah.'

'Stand up.' I got Glassbrook on his feet. He kicked the mess of chips and wrapper on the van floor with his boots, itched his greasy tash on his shoulder – his mouth painting everything red.

I walked him to the back doors – counted Ivey's footsteps outside as he made his way round.

Streetlight split the doors. Fresh air.

Glassbrook went first: 'Let im get on with it, Ivey! Fuckin let im get out n breathe.'

'Always smooth in the field – ay, Glassbrook.' Ivey stepped aside for me – tissue balls in his nose, trying to be full of it and frown at the same time.

I jumped out the van. 'There's more grub in there if any o you fancy it. Cook it tomorrow. Seafood breakfast. Job done.'

'Bane, I'll call yer,' Glassbrook said, leering out the van. This fat bastard in his own handcuffs – his gob open, choppers like broken dishes. *Foreign hotel maids doing their job.* 'I'll call yer,' he said again. Desperate as sin.

I turned my back and took a left off the side street – head swimming with nonsense.

Deansgate and Frank were a sprint away.

21

FRIENDS IN HIGH PLACES

I WALKED UP the line.

They were battery hens. Clutch bags under one wing, hairspray nests, carrot-coloured boots. A couple of them even had on feather frocks. I glanced back from nearer the entrance: single file down the street, sucking fags, hugging wall – past the corner and beyond.

There were a few Suits as well, hopping out of taxis to jump the queue – the Kitchen Club rats had found their next ship.

Billyclub opened last February and the fuss still hadn't died down. The manager was a wet leaf – I'd met him the once, on launch night. I remember our Frank's teeth clamped together for a big smile, his mutton chops waxed down. I remember our Frank's hand shaking his too hard, wishing him all the best – eyes shooting daggers throughout. But then Billyclub started doing mega-expensive grub. Opening at dinnertime. Some daft lad told Frank that you had to book three weeks ahead to get a table, sometimes four. Once again, Frank was over the moon. The bloke who told him lost a finger in the back of the Britton, chopping onions. Plenty of tears.

It was rowdy by the main doors. There were gobby birds having their handbags checked by the bouncers. One bouncer saw me as I pushed past.

'Jamie?' I said. No coincidence. I kept one hand in my pocket, hid my skinned knuckles.

'Bane! Lookin a bit rough, lad. Alright? Ow's tricks?'

'Not too bad.'

'What's wiv shiner?'

I touched my eye. 'Mugged for me jacket,' I said.

Jamie laughed. 'Shit. Where was this?'

'Macclesfield-way.' I'd packed today's four scraps into one.

'Fuck me. Goes to show, gotta be careful anywhere these days.'

I said: 'You were quick gettin yourself a new gig.'

'Dint waste time, no point, right? Ah work out wiv a couple o the fellers ere. Got us sorted.'

'Fair play.'

'Tell yer though, am still avin nightmares bout Friday. One minute am gettin radioed to the front to elp sort out some piss ed, nex thing the place is in flames. Punters stampedin out the door. Dint even see *you* come out, mate.' He was mashed on charlie, again – face wet, tongue wagging on and on.

'Sorry bout Shell,' I said.

'Yeah, well. Gone now, ant she – like im. Formby. Now they know it's bloody murder, the rumours be flyin, mate. Am tellin yer – Formby gets snuffed by some mystery men – it's shit news fer anyone wanted a bit o—'

'What's it like in?' I said – questions to avoid questions.

Jamie turned his head. 'What, in ere? Buzzin. It's fuckin raz in there tonight, mate. Plennyofanny.'

'How much?'

'Fifteen. Guest-list only.'

'Sounds a racket.'

'Nah, they play the proper stuff tonight,' he said. 'Our kid's DJin at one.'

'I meant that's fuckin steep.' Not that I was short, mind.

'Oh right, yeah – bit dear, init? Lucky yer on VIP, mate.'

'Am I?'

Jamie turned to the next bouncer. He was busy feeling up some bird in a short-sleeved jacket – her arms out like a scarecrow. 'Yer seen Ryan, mate?' Jamie said. The bouncer nodded – cocked his head to point him out.

This Ryan passed Jamie the guest-list. Jamie didn't take it – he just tapped the clipboard, scanning it upside down with his finger, lightning quick. Just for show. Good form.

'Yeah, go on, mate,' he said to me. 'Av a top one.'

I said: 'In a bit, mate,' gave him a pat and stepped inside. Easy enough.

A young bird with too much perfume on her tits smiled and branded my hand. She let it go and stamped the next. I looked down at the smudge of ink. Livestock.

A Voodoo Ray remix hit me as I went in – bassline pumping through my chest like poisoned air. I was fucking spent. I made it to the bar and pinched a stool.

'What yer avin, love?' A short bird, a curvy twelve, everything on show – heavy jewellery on her fingers, neck, down her frock. She looked a bit like our Jan with a bleach perm.

'Kaliber.'

'Don't do Kaliber,' she said.

'Don't do Kaliber?'

'Pardon?' She bent over the bar top – necklaces swinging – she cupped her left ear.

I said: 'Give us a Pepsi, love. Half-pint. No ice.'

She put a black serviette down and an empty glass on top of it. She pulled the hose up on the bar and pointed the nozzle in the glass. She pressed the trigger. 'Diet Coke', she went. 'Three quid.'

I put my hands up. 'You got the right case?'

'Pardon?'

I finished the drink at the bar.

Billyclub had another room to fill but the place was already rammed. The DJ was playing 'Dream Attack' – somebody's Manchester classics. Nobody was dancing yet. There was a knot of birds stood chatting next to me while they were being served. One dropped her change as she paid for a Malibu. I got off my stool to pick it up for her, but she went down as well. Chunky heels. Shiny silver frock. She'd already managed to get ladders in her stockings.

She looked up at me, grinning. 'Ta. Oo yer ere wiv, lovey?'

'Mates,' I said.

We stood up together.

'Can yer get us in VIP?'

'Where?' I said.

'Over there.' She pointed to the far end. Between the bodies, I spied the table service behind the rope.

The New Order tune faded out – Manchester with it. Mark Morrison, 'Return of the Mack,' replaced it.

'See what yer can do, love,' she said, pecking my cheek. One of her mates tapped her on the shoulder. They all took their drinks, made a daisy chain and clopped over to the dance floor.

Ladders tossed me a wave.

I got off my stool and was swallowed by the traffic of dancers. They spat me out at the other end by the VIP section. Two slapheads with earpieces were guarding the rope. I leant against the back wall and watched from a stretch away.

A fancy mob on the long plush sofas. Three tables with buckets of ice and decent bubbly. A bloke in his forties at the middle table looked like Top Dog. He had silver temples – blue under the swirly lights. He did the talking. The rest did the nodding. A waitress put a fresh bottle on the table and touched his arm, interrupting him.

I read her lips: *Would you like me to pour it?*

He closed his fingers around her wrist and lifted it up like the grabber inside those cuddly-toy machines in arcades. He dropped her hand down onto the arm of the sofa.

The bloke opposite took the fresh bubbly and poured it out, first glass went to Silver. He flashed a daft chunky watch – probably Rolex. Naff and showy. Worse than Frank's. He was wearing an open shirt, a fat chain around his neck – too nasty to be fake. No fucking class.

Silver sat back with his drink. Birthmark was next to him – bare legs folded. He rapped his fingers on her knee and then left it alone. She didn't seem too mithered. Maybe this Silver fucker was Lance. But no sign of Emil. I looked back to her:

The Doll Princess.

A wet skeleton – no skin in the cold club lights. Big eyes sucking in everything, letting none of it back out. She didn't clock me once.

Gents.

I did my hands first. Then face. I sniffed the ice water – taps on full, my head in the sink – swilling the rage out of my gob.

A black feller handed me two paper towels. He was perched by the far sink, men's perfume knock-offs next to him. The counter wore his hat upside down, collecting quids. He read a paperback in one hand: *How To Improve Your Written English*.

'Any good?' I said, drying my face.

'Not so bad,' he said.

I pointed to the smellies. 'What you recommend?'

'For you? For you – this one.' He put the book down, picked up a bottle and squirted it in front me. 'Good, yes?'

'Go for it.' He handed me the bottle.

Another punter came in for a piss and left without washing his hands.

I added a coin to the pile.

When I turned around, she was leaning on a cubicle door, just like that. Loose olive frock. Bare legs like pins. Tarty Eurotrash earrings. Hair slicked back, tamed. What was it about me and her and bathrooms?

I put a twenty in the hat, without saying a word, without taking my eyes off her, and she gave the attendant a nod with some blank authority. He left out the main door – book in hand.

Her tongue tasted sugary and bitter like aniseed, scrubbing at my teeth. She spat into my gob. Her throat made ugly sounds. I swallowed, felt her teeth in my bottom lip – before we let go.

I locked us in a cubicle and she pushed me back against the cistern and got my cock out – pulled her frock up, tugged her knickers down – snapping them off her heels. She was all angles. Her hips were bony – wider than they first looked. She showed it me

– spread it over my thighs. We fucked like sensible animals. Noisy and fast and bolshie. No rhythms. Just the slosh of cunt. I pulled her frock-straps down off her shoulders, down past her tits. I bit her. She bit me. I sucked the crown birthmark on her arm. We shagged like this for another minute – panting, faces together, until there was nothing left.

We heard the main door swing open. Music came in and went away again. Blokes' voices. Arguing over rounds.

She peeled the side of her face off mine first, but kept me inside her. Her eyes were dry, hard to read, and the pale skin on her chest had turned pink like a rash.

22

FUMES

RAZDAN'S GARAGE. JUST gone twelve. A couple of the Asian lads let on to me in the yard.

'Maz about?' I said as one came out from the office – tatty green overalls, oil-stained Prada cap, knock-off trainers, a mug of tea in his hand.

'Maz?' he said, then turned his head and barked up the yard to a couple of lads gabbing by the tyre stacks. They had a little rally in their own language before he looked back at me, took a gulp of his brew and went: 'Fuck knows, mate. Might be still sprayin up in back room. Not seen im in time.'

'Cheers.' I went in the empty garage and spotted my motor parked up by the wall and had a quick look at the new bumper. The dents were out of the side panel. Good as new.

The wooden doors to the back room were locked. It

was chilly this end of the unit, even though it was another scorcher outside. I cupped my hands over my eyes, pressed my face up to the small square window. No Maz, just one great cloud of paint. I could hear the noise of the sprayer, see a glow from a mobile paraffin heater humming on the floor, the glint of a fag whizzing round by itself – flying like a pissed Tinkerbell as he went about the job. Maz, the bloody lump of lard – totally hidden by the paint mist.

I banged on the window with the knuckles of my good hand and shouted: 'Oi' – giving the bottom of the doors a boot. 'Maz!' Rubber sole scuffed the wood. I made the doors rattle.

The sprayer switched off. I could hear music on in there as well. Naff radio rap. Nothing decent. That Westwood wanker trying his best.

'Keep yer fuckin air on!' Maz said, unlocking the door. It opened and he stood there, fag in gob, no mask on. 'Oh, alright Bane. Motor's ready.'

Cheap paint fumes burnt my throat – smelled worse than the Chemist's lab. Maz wore an XXL all-in-one. He was covered in the stuff.

I said: 'You do realise you're inside a fuckin bomb, mate?'

Maz shrugged and dropped his cig on the concrete floor between us. I stamped it out. 'Nah, don't worry,' he said, 'Al be right.'

The next song came on the radio. 'If I Ruled the World'. Lauryn you could forgive him for, but that poppy bollocks just wasn't Nasty Nas.

I nodded to the heater. 'Get that off. Must be mad. Barmy bugger.'

Maz went back and unplugged it, unplugged the cassette radio as well. He had four car doors off, tipped against the wall. They were going from white to City-blue.

'Yer seen it?' he said.

'Me car? Yeah, just now. Looks alright.'

'Does dunit? Where's that one ah lent yer?' he said, picking up a rag and coming back.

'In the yard,' I said. He was just wiping wet paint round his forehead with the rag, working it into his hands, making a right mess of it.

'There's a touch o blood on the backseat. Vac'd it fer yer, though.'

'Ay?' He looked at his blue hands. 'Bastard – need to grab us some turps.'

'Maz, how come you never said it was nicked?'

'Yer what?' He stopped rubbing the paint in.

'The car.'

'Fuckin ell – am sorry, mate. Yer get stopped?'

'Sort of. Would've been nice to know.'

Maz shook his head, blew lots of air out of his chubby cheeks. He knew he'd fucked up: 'Don't know what to tell yer, mate,' he said. 'Am dead sorry, mate.'

'You've said.'

Maz unstrapped the collar of his all-in-one and unzipped it. He tugged and jiggled it down him, had a bit of grief when it came to his waistline. It was like watching a walrus trying to shed its skin. He stepped out of it in the end and gave me a little bow. He had his mechanic overalls on underneath.

I said: 'Smooth job.'

'Ay, somebody come askin round bout yer yesterday. Wanted to know oo's name yer motor was in.'

'You tell um it was a company car? Belongs to a Mister F. Holland?'

'Nah. Think ee knew already. Ee were after yer, though. Told im nowt.' Maz's eyes went watery. 'Look, mate – am dead fuckin sorry bout the ot motor. Tell yer what, fancy a brew?'

'Yeah, go on,' I said.

Maz gulped his from a chipped Kit-Kat mug in the pokey office. 'Ow was yer weekend, then?' he said, big arse on little swivel chair.

'Standard,' I said, giving mine a go – still piping hot. I could smell the off milk in it.

'Get up to owt yesterday?'

I put the dirty Ford mug back on the dirty Ford coaster on the desk. 'This n that,' I said.

'So yer gunna tell us or what, mate? Oo give yer black eye?'

'Where's that good-lookin bird that does the phones?'

'Kam? That's me cousin. She's gettin er dinner. Frank was it? Yer eye?'

'How's your sister?'

'Fuckin ell Bane, oo did it?'

'It's not bout Frank. This is another do.'

'Yuv bin busy. Busier than yer lettin on, sound of it.'

'Do you remember Alice?'

'Oo?'

'Alice. Alice Willows.'

'. . . ?'

'Lived round our way, back in the schooldays.'

'Red ed?'

'No.'

'She a looker?'

'Yeah. No. Alright. Not your sort.'

'Then sorry, mate. Ah don't. Why?'

I thought about telling him about the funeral but didn't. 'Never mind.'

Maz polished off his brew, *ahhhd* like it was sip one of pint one after a hard day's graft. Not that Maz had a local he wanted to be seen in. He plonked the empty mug down on the side and stood up, steering the conversation back round to Frank: 'Ah eard ee's got the lads bloody gunnin fer yer, mate. Ad fuck off fer a bit if ah were enry Bane. This is Bad Elvis. The King—'

Illegal Immigrants R Us.

'—Frank. Ee means bloody business.'

'Show business?'

Maz laughed. 'See the jacket's doin the job.'

I touched my collar, folded the tartan lining down. 'No complaints.'

Maz opened the bottom drawer of the filing cabinet – pulled out seven or eight long flat rectangles. He kicked the drawer, made it clatter shut – neatened the pile in his hand and turned them over. He showed me the one on top. Car number plates.

I took the bundle and spread them out on the desk, gave my tea a second chance – a bad brew.

'Fer yer motor, mate,' he said. 'Do the job, won't it? Do um now. Tek a minute.'

'For what?'

'Fer nowt.'

'Y'know I might need your help in the week, Maz. Maybe one evenin. Not sure yet. You gunna be around?'

'Should be, yeah. Tomorra ah will be, anyroad. Trouble?'

I put my finger on a number plate and scooped the set up off the desk. Maz was eyeing my grazed knuckles when I passed them over.

He said: 'Oo's ad a knuckle sandwich?'

Good hand touched bad temple. I pushed the bruise next to my eye. 'Not the feller who gave us this.'

'Not seen yer like this fer time. Yer into summat fuckin shady, mate?'

I headed out the office, back into the garage. 'Maz, can you sort us some petrol? Couple o empty bottles.'

Maz shouted: 'Yeah, can do. Ay, finished wiv yer tea? Ant touched it.'

'You still can't make a brew.'

I got inside and adjusted the rear-view – caught my reflection, forgot to blink. Glassbrook's mobile was still in my pocket and I took it out, saw the battery bar and put it in the glovebox.

Keys in the ignition, gearstick in reverse, dash clock saying dinnertime. I'd have to grab some grub afterwards – it was already time to meet her.

23

FURNITURE SALE

I FOUND A space, parked on Swan Street. No neon, just a hand-painted sign by a tatty double door. The archway was donkey's old – worn-down cherubs carved in the brickwork. *Porn-Porn-Porn*. Nobody could moan they were misled. It was a dodgy little backstreet theatre playing all the hard smut. Bit of a fucking relic, really. Cheap and nasty, heavy on the nasty. Flyers for specialist imported stuff nailed to the doors – floating somebody's boat.

A goth girl let me in on her way out. Lace lilac crop-top, mini leather skirt. Great white legs stretching out black fishnets. She marched off down the sunny street and I took my step into the dark.

Another bird was sat behind a box-office cage in the gloom. Thirty-odd, bored out of her skull, the chorus to 'Little Red Corvette' fizzing out of her Walkman headphones. There were long lit candles tattooed up her forearms, top-shelf mags stacked up on both sides of the counter. She made me cough up a tenner for the Monday matinee. No tea served.

'You into Prince?' I said.

She handed me a ticket. 'No wanking,' she said.

No flasher macs but it was the typical grubby lot inside. The place stank of filth – muggy with all the sweating. I pulled at my shirt to let my skin breathe.

The place was cosy enough. There were about twelve seats to a row, ten rows in all and not a bad turnout, even in this heat. It had a high ceiling – the back projector light seemed half a mile up. I cleared my throat and sat down second from the back row. Someone caught my feet as I pushed past. 'Watch yourself,' I said. A few lads on the front row shot their heads round and shushed me, faces sweating. Pervy scrubbers. I smiled, tipped an invisible flat-cap and gave a big Norman Wisdom wink.

The next picture started – a hard European number called *Credentialist Society and the Self-Appointed Missionary. MCMLXXXIX.* Must have been an arty one. The credits were cut up with shagging, rough stuff but fake, still not my speed.

Snot-coloured light from the screen lit up the marker-pen posters on the wall, told me I was in store for a double bill with *Qarînah!*

Two blokes were sat in front of me. One said: 'Er tits are dead wonky. Them aren't real – are they?'

The other one said: 'What?'

'Er tits.'

'Give er a ring n tell er. Ow do I know?'

'Fuck off. Were jus sayin.'

Front Row called back: 'Oi loud moufs, yer can fuck off!'

'Wanker!'

'Too bloody right!'

Cue a shushing free-for-all that went on and on and on.

She sidled up the row towards me in the middle of this racket. No light, but I could tell it was her. Her arse made it to the seat next to mine. I recognised the smell of her sweat, thought about kissing her, kissed her, tried for mouth – managed her throat. She didn't take offence.

After a minute, she led me out of the side exit and down a short corridor – her stilettos noisy in the dark. At the end of the corridor, I helped her open a dodgy fire door – blinking when sunshine hit my eyes.

I said: 'Bloody hell,' grinning through the pain.

Shades on, she wasn't mithered.

When I could take the light, I saw we were in a little square courtyard filled with bin bags and bits of wood. Dark wood, not junk – antique cabinet furniture that had been smashed to bits. We crossed the courtyard and she opened an iron gate and ran up a steep flight of stairs, quick and careful in those heels. I followed. The steps finished with another tatty door. She knocked on the door and waited and then she looked back at me for the first time.

I looked at her.

Pixie cheekbones. Gorgeous angry gob. There was a touch of sweat on her neck and forehead. Her hair was up, no mousse, blonder by day, sunglasses on top. She had a half-sleeve blouse – Daz white, black handbag on one shoulder. Skintight denim. No belt. Hips full. Legs lean. Feet safe in fuck-off high heels. She came over and stopped in front of me, a bit close for comfort. Those eyes looked grey for the minute. It all looked different in the daytime – not quite warm-blooded, but she'd altered her game.

'You've scrubbed up well, love,' I said, feeling a right pillock.

She smiled, stopped smiling, went back to the door and knocked again. We waited.

'Boo,' I said. She turned – eyes wide open. There was another smile but it didn't go full term.

'Come on,' she said to me, or maybe she meant the door. 'Come on.'

I said: 'Ta.'

'What?' she said.

'Thanks.'

'Why?'

'Savin me arse on Friday. Been kicked a few times since, though.'

'You're welcome.' She had a weak voice that over-pronounced its words. No accent. Nothing I could place. But it was fucking Queen's English. She slapped the door hard with her whole hand, stamped a heel into the floor.

Keys rattled. Locks unlocked.

A weedy feller in a stained vest and Umbro trackies stood in the doorway. There were mean scars up and down his arms, a few tats. He coughed and moved out of her way and we went inside. He reeked of cider, was in need of a decent shave, had a nose that'd seen a few fists.

It was a grotty little den inside. Jungle hot. Even worse than the smut house. The feller in trackies took us into this shit-tip of a front room. These were odd digs: frilly lampshades and paintings of windmills in antique frames. One ruined china rug on the floor – two more rolled with tape, propped up against the wall.

'We stoppin for a brew?' I said.

Fruit-juice cartons were in a dirty big ashtray on the coffee table. The back wall of the front room was knocked through to a wider dining room, how much wider I couldn't see from this angle. I clocked some freezer bags filled with gear – piled up like a wonky Jenga tower over on a breakfast table, a shut window directly above it.

Back in the front room, there was a bird lying on a chesterfield couch. I recognised her – boyish haircut, grey freckles down her back. An orange plastic straw stuck to her lip fluttered as she breathed. She was stretched out flat, bare arm and bare foot dangling over the carpet. Platform shoes nearby. She wore a Minnie Mouse vest back-to-front – no knickers on.

There was an empty syringe arrowed in her pale arse.

I pulled it out and dropped it on the coffee table into a pool of Um Bongo. I looked to the feller. The Doll Princess was stood next to him, going through her handbag.

'She bad by hot weather.' He showed me ten fingers. 'For fuck.'

'Ten quid?' I said.

He nodded, came closer. He showed me his teeth and the gaps where he was missing a couple. I thought of Glassbrook.

He said: 'Ten – ten, yes?'

I poked his chest with two fingers to get his reeking gob out of my face. He'd been bombing more than cider. When he sat back in a chesterfield chair, I sat on the couch and touched the girl's hair: 'We right, love?'

No joy. She was well out of it.

I said: 'Does somebody fancy openin a window?'

The feller shook his head, said something that sounded like a no more times than I needed to hear.

'Think the poor cow's fuckin off anywhere on her own? Open the window. Now. Can't breathe in here.'

He gozzed on the china rug, wiped his chin, got up and went through to the dining room and did as he was told. An honest breeze came through into the front room. You could hear some kids yelling up the street. He had second thoughts and shut the window again.

The Doll Princess called out to him from the other side of the flat. We had a moment of silence. Then he called her something. He was asking her to come over to him but she wouldn't budge. They spoke a bit more in his language, kept up their little staring contest.

She came out on top. Money was the magic word. She held out the fist of cash at arm's length, standing up straight, her feet apart, looking him dead in the face – hers was stone. He left the window and came over, caught his foot on the edge of the china rug and tripped.

I felt the girl stir on the couch next to me.

He put his hand out to take the cash and she dropped the ball of notes before he'd gotten under it. He fell to his knees again, laughing – plucked the tenners up, one at a time, making a show of it. Then he said something to her, still kneeling at her feet. She nodded, chin up – eyes low – and he got up and tramped out of the room.

'Is he fuckin doolally?' I said.

'Do you remember her?' she said to me.

'Who? This one?' I said, my fingers still in her hair. 'She was one o the broken dolls at Kitchen Club on Friday. Wasn't she?'

The Doll Princess said: 'Yes.'

I said: 'Spent an evenin on Formby's lap. Poor cow.'

The Doll Princess came to the sofa and put her hand on the bird's ankle, rubbed her dangling foot.

'Poor cow,' she repeated slowly.

The girl got colder.

She let go of the girl's foot as the bloke reappeared, a button bag of something or other in his hand.

He gave it her and she pushed it in the zip pocket

of her handbag. The bird on the sofa coughed and I turned my head. Her toes clenched up.

I said: 'Get your dancin shoes on, dozy. We're off. Come on, love.' I tapped her face, softly, and pushed her upright. It was an effort, she was dead weight.

'Leave her,' the Doll Princess went, already heading for the front door.

I said: 'You want us to leave her? Like this? She's a right fuckin state.'

'We've got what we came for,' she said.

'Ay?'

'Come on.'

I stood up and went over to the window in the other room and opened it again – looked out but the kids had gone. The sun was blinding, reflecting white off the windows down the high street. Two cars passed. In the flat, a brown door was open to the left, showing me a kitchenette – to my right, more birds on antique furniture. Two of them. They looked like they were waiting for the dentist. Eyes open, watching nothing. Not even each other. I recognised them both from Friday night. One was lying down on a padded couch, creasing up her minidress – fluffy blonde hair stuck to her forehead, no tits, bruised shins. The other one wasn't quite sitting up but lolling in between. She was in a short-short skirt, missing a top, just a damp yellow bra on her chest, supporting nothing much. Neither of them were the kind of totty you'd be mithered to see on a trampoline.

I spotted a Zippo on the breakfast table and took it,

my hand knocking over the coke-bag tower by accident. Thumb down, the flame sparked first go and I waved it out in front of one of the birds. 'Fuck me,' I said, seeing her dead eyes track the flame this-way-and-that-way, sweat dripping faster. I was a snake charmer. It was just like with the Chemist's bird, Tara. Spooky shit.

'Ten,' the feller said again. I saw him as a blur in the corner of my eye, near that open window.

I said: 'Don't even think about it, mate, or I'll put your fuckin head through it.'

'Ten,' he said.

'I can still count.'

'No. Ten. For both.'

And he pointed at them.

I let the Zippo flame die and lifted the girl in the skirt onto her feet. She stood there without my help, stiff, sort of swaying.

The feller pulled a dock-off flick knife out of his trackies – the blade a good size – it was like something that belonged to an old Teddy-boy greaser. Blade out, he pointed it at me, tilting his head for me to put her back down on the furniture.

I took out the gun, pointed it at him. 'Oi.'

The Doll Princess came into the room. Her big eyes caught the reflected sunlight from the window, bouncing off the flick-knife blade. She squinted – put her arm up. Her half sleeves were rolled high, as if she was ready for a scrap. I could just about see the crown birthmark, showing through the material.

The knife disappeared back in the trackies. I still

had the little shooter in his face. Emil's CZ 99. He just looked at me, respectful, sober. After a couple of seconds, I felt daft so I put it away.

'How much to buy?' I said.

He turned back to say something to the Doll Princess and then looked at me again. 'For both?'

'The three of um,' I said.

'Four thousand each. Will have more tomorrow.'

'More birds?'

The Doll Princess took me by the elbow and led me out the flat. 'More birds,' he said, following us to the door.

24

EVERY BUGGER'S DEAD

'WHAT'S WRONG WITH your hand?' she said, sunglasses back on.

'It's the wrist,' I said, twisting it back and forth. 'Fucked it up tryna shoot someone.'

'That's why Emil is angry.'

I stopped still before we got to the car. She carried on trotting down the pavement but her head turned after a second.

I didn't know where to start.

In the car, she told me where we were going, where it'd be safe to have a nice chat, she said we wouldn't be followed. We'd even stop off for flowers along the way.

We drove in silence for a good quarter of an hour without the radio on and then she said: 'I worked there before this.'

'What? Back there?'

'Yes.'

'One o those broken dolls.'

'When I first came here.'

'What are you then? Polish?'

'No. Not Polish.'

'Not many of um about. Our Frank says there will be. Says the foreigners are the future. Three pillars o the European Union n all that. He only hires the ones with the dodgy visas. The illegals. No papers. He can do what he likes. He fuckin loves the power. N that proper continental food.'

'The crow won't peck out the eye of another crow.'

'Yes, love – it fuckin well will.' I put my foot down after passing a set of lights. 'Frank used to say since the Sovey Union went tits up – Eastern Europe's gone sex mad. Gangsters, porno, prozzies – everyone's barmy for it. What you reckon?'

With her dark sunglasses on, I couldn't tell if she was looking at me or the road ahead.

'Few o Frank's chefs taught us some Polish dishes. Only basic, like – just one or two.'

'I'm not Polish,' she said.

I said: 'Yeah. Sorry.'

'You talk so much about Frank. Is he your father?'

I laughed. 'Ex-boss. Bad appraisal. Wants my head on a stick.'

'Frank Holland?'

'You know more than you let on,' I said, 'but we already knew that. Didn't we, love?'

She said nothing, picked her handbag up from the footwell and took out what she'd bought from the pimp. 'This is datura.'

I said: 'That burundanga when it's at home?'

She nodded. 'Essentially.' She broke the word up into three. It sounded strange enough coming out of her mouth. 'Are you worried?' she said – face to the window.

Was I? She wouldn't save my arse one night to get it fucked now.

'No,' I said. 'Not worried. Are you?'

Her head turned, lips moved. '*For* you,' she said.

Up Barlow Moor Road. Southern Cem. I let her out to grab a bunch of flowers from a lad with a bum bag, selling them from green buckets by the side of the road. I drove on and pinched a space. She was already marching down with them in one hand – this long shadow well ahead of her on the pavement slabs.

The white flowers were tulips. The sunshine had been good to them.

'We can go in this way – it's quieter,' she said.

I saw myself nod inside her big sunglasses and we started to walk.

'Some foreigner, you. Speak better English than us.'

Thin eyebrows went up. Disappeared again. 'I do,' she said – but I couldn't tell if she'd meant it to be a question.

'You don't sound fresh off the boat.'

'I've been here one year.'

I asked her again: 'Where you from, then?'

We went through the entrance, carried straight onto the criss-cross of footpaths – grass and gravestones on both sides, mangy bunny-rabbit traffic in front.

Still trying: 'Can tell us, love. Nobody's listenin, these buggers are all dead.'

Somehow, it was this that got another legit smile. 'All of them are dead,' she repeated – turning her head, scouting round. But she wasn't going to tell me.

'You learnt English quick,' I said.

'I can speak four languages.'

'Showin off are we?'

'But you only learn the words you need first.'

'We all have to survive, ay?'

'My brother taught me English before I came to this country.'

'This Lance. He bring you over, did he?'

Nothing.

'Emil?'

'No,' she said, moving the bunch into her other fist. There was one droopy flower on the outside, dry, half-dead – it spoilt the whole lot.

'Someone did,' I said. 'To work?'

'Yes.' She crushed the wrapping paper tightly, plucked out the bad flower and tossed it in the soil gutter of a passing grave.

'What do they tell you on the other end? You're all gunna end up fuckin waitresses n childminders? Some o you must o known. Specially you. I look at you n think this one's a sharp tool, sharp as fuck, n

I start wonderin if I really wanna know what it's all about.'

'Not one of us had a choice.'

'Worse back home, was it? Worse than this?'

She took her shades off – wiped then back over her hair, eyes blinked and steadied on me. 'Now? Was much worse *then*.' They were the colour of old roof slate. Empty, dry, clever.

'What happened? Got lucky? This twat Lance see some potential and pick you out for his steady?'

Her face zoomed closer and I thought I'd pushed it too far but she kissed me on the mouth, quickly. 'And now I have picked you.'

'Lucky me.'

She took a left and we went up the next footpath, the gravel sounded hard on her shoes.

I said: 'So now you're more than survivin. Unlike the rest o them poor cows – the ones still in that smiler's flat.' I waited for her to speak but she didn't so I tried something else: 'Tell us about him. The Balkan feller with the tats. Emil.'

I waited.

Eventually: 'He works with Lance.' She showed me the back of her head as we watched a couple of young kiddies chasing bunnies about. The kiddies' folks stood by a grave in the baby garden, ready to dish them a bollocking. 'Emil protects him,' she said. 'Protects his business. In London. Up here. Abroad. Everywhere.'

'He runs the show? Everythin?'

'Not everything.'

'Lance is top dog?'

'Yes.'

'Was he the flash tosser at Billyclub last night? Grey temples – greasy ponce – Rolex – didn't like bein touched?'

'Yes. He can't stand it.'

'Even with you?'

'Sometimes.' She was actually looking for a grave, counting each headstone.

'Jammy for you, then – ay? Emil's had a go, though – seen the pictures.'

She swallowed – said out to the dead: 'You don't know what you're talking about.'

'That why your Lance isn't too mithered? Puffter? Or is it one o them *mates share* arrangements?'

She didn't hear me. She came off the path and dropped the flowers on a grave – the headstone was blank, hadn't been engraved. I came over. 'Pigs, they just let um get on with it? Trafficking birds, shooters, the lot?'

'They let you get on with it.' She bent over to arrange the flowers, patting them down.

'I'm a lad from Wythie that muscles folks for a bit o cash. I sell some E every now n then. Some fuckin gear. Nothin heavy. I've never done any real time. These boys are in a different fuckin league.'

Little shoulders shrugged up – her back to me. She was still working on the flowers.

I kept things quiet: 'You were after dosh, simple as, robbin that daft cow, Safir, blind. But kidnappin Abdul Muhsi was a bit extreme. Fuck me. None of it's been discreet. So who fucked it up? N how did my Alice get involved?'

She looked up, still crouching down. 'Who?'

'The other prozzie. The one that bimmer tossed out on Stockport Road when your lot was done with her.'

'Your friend?' she said.

'Aye.'

'There was a boy. Did you know him?'

Gerry? 'Nah, but I bloody feel like I do – heard enough bout the lad.'

She held a hand out for mine and I helped her stand. 'I like you,' she said. 'You're angry about what happened to your friend even though it won't do any good.'

'What won't?'

'Trying to kill who killed her.'

'Who killed her?'

'I don't know. Nobody you can do anything to.'

'But you do know, love. Just tell us who it was? I've been right from the start, haven't I? Emil, yeah? N your fuckin fancy man?'

'Who killed her,' she said back to me. Maybe a question.

'That's all I'm askin for, love. Just the truth. Was. It. Fuckin. Them?'

'Yes. Probably.'

'I can't be doin with this.'

'You can't be doing with what?'

'Fuck it. Never mind.' A family pushing a buggy came up the path nearby, the toddler holding the flowers, too well-behaved. I waited for them to pass out of earshot.

'So over time this Lance – he's extended your leash. Let's you go on walkies all by yourself?'

'Yes.'

'So either he's just dense n a penny short, which goes off with everythin you've just been tellin us, or you, love, are about gettin me fucked. So what did you tell him?'

'They buried my son here. He lets me visit him whenever I want.'

I looked at the unmarked stone. It was new, not too weathered. 'You had a kid? You?'

'Yes.'

'How old was he?'

'Eight.'

Christ. 'When he . . . ?'

She nodded.

'He came over, then . . . with you from wherever?'

Still nodding.

'Then Emil bought us,' she said – on the move again.

'What happened to the lad?'

She wouldn't say. I had another dozen questions but I let the Q&A round pass, since she was itching to get off. 'You off?' I said.

'What?'

'You goin now?'

'Yes.'

'I'll need to see you again.'

She looked a tad nervous for the first time since we'd met. The shades went back on. We started walking out a different way.

'When can I see you?' I said.

'Do you have a phone?'

I dug out Glassbrook's mobile and she put a phone number in it and gave it me back.

'Look, what do you think I can do for you? Love, you don't need us. You could fuck off whenever you like. I think it's bollocks. So I got a bit ugly with you the other night – you realise I'm not battin for Formby or your lot and you think I might be worth havin in goal. Why? What you cookin up for Lance?'

'There's an auction tonight. Twelve-thirty. Pomona Docks.'

'Don't piss us about.'

She was moving faster than me, almost out the gates. 'Oi,' I said, until her heels stopped trotting. 'You think I need the aggro? Love, you're confusin us with the good lad. I don't give a fuck, me. I'm the rum lot in our family. The old man doesn't even send us a Christmas card. I get fuck all.'

'You want to help them. I saw you. I saw you today.'

A black BMW was waiting on Nell Lane. 7-Series, tinted glass, flash custom wheels. The kind our Maz went for. I kept out of sight, caught the middle two letters of a private plate as it sped off with her in the backseat.

My pocket was ringing.

'Hello?' I said, phone to my ear, looking round 360.

'Oo's *that* dollybird?' He had a lisp.

'Your mam.'

'Let's av a talk.' It was more of a whistle.

'Let's.'

'Wherever yer feel comfortable, laddie.'

But he was still kissing arse.

25

SALT IN ME WOUNDS

EDNA'S CAFF. RADIO on loud. It was Suede's 'We are the Pigs' over the racket of spitting fryers and allsorts on the stoves.

There were two old-timers sat on the furthest table, wearing fake camel hairs in this weather, indoors, playing a game of dominoes. The bloke with his back to the wall was chewing chuddy like it was keeping his heart ticking. The bloke nearest me had his dominoes all lined up on the flat of one hand.

'Am bitin me fingers,' Sandy said to me, watching them, and then smiling when I did.

'Bacon butty n a packet o Golden Wonder for danger boy, here,' Dougie Glassbrook said, slapping the counter.

Sandy rolled her eyes. 'What flavour, love?' Her hair was up, so damp with sweat it looked like she'd come out the shower.

'What flavour?' Glassbrook asked me.

'Same as you, mate,' I said.

'Same as me? I can't do crisps. Can't even av ot drinks.' Glassbrook whistled – pointing at his gob, like I'd forgotten where the shit came out of him. There were more gaps in his teeth than I remembered making.

'Took um out quick,' I said.

'This mornin,' he said – his top lip still a bit swollen with anaesthetic, pushing out his big tash. 'Two of um were black to the root.'

'Told you, didn't I?' I said, putting my Harrington on a chair and sitting at a table. 'Don't forget the brew.'

He paid, came over with the bag of crisps and sat down opposite. 'She's bringin um over.' He leant over the table. 'She's a bit alright, int she?'

I stared him out.

'Badge says Sandy,' he said. 'But where's Edna? That's what I wanna know.'

Space 'Neighbourhood' came on next, no chance. Sandy flicked stations – 'Cigarettes and Alcohol' – she couldn't seem to find anything decent so just switched it off. The fryers got noisier.

'Where's the Lundon lad?' I said.

'Ivey?'

'That's the one.'

'On the job.'

'What's this then?'

'Different job.'

'What's he then?'

'D.I.S.'

'Sounds well-to-do. But lets you give him a bollockin, does he?'

'Nah. Give n take, it is. Ee's not from round here, ee's Whitehall – which means ee likes wearin is paisley tie when ee's givin um a good kickin. But ee's alright, yer know? Yugoslav Crisis Cell? Ever read bout that one in your papers?'

'Let's get on with this, ay? Appeal to me good side, Glassbrook. You don't know us – might even have one.'

'What's the rush? Butties to come yet.' He called out to Sandy. 'Scuze us, can yer put that one back on, lovey.'

'Radio?'

'Aye. If yer could.'

Sandy growled. I could see the sweat shining on her cheeks. 'Drive me bloody mad, them do.'

'Please.'

Sandy turned it back on.

And God gave us the Gallaghers.

'Brassy buggers, these,' Glassbrook said to me. Then he talked quietly: 'Bane, there's nowt in the basement o that keep-fit club. The Florencia? The Fuck-all. No Muhsi. No drugs. No guns. They ad a bit of a do wiv a gas leak but there's nowt.'

'Who owns it?' I said.

'Yer know oo. Ee's got a few abroad as well. It's all legit.'

'Ay?' I said.

Glassbrook tried for a sigh but whistled through his teeth instead.

'CCTV, security cams? You check um, did you?' But I knew I was talking bollocks.

He was still whistling.

'They're traffickin birds from Europe,' I said.

'Yer what?'

'Lorry loads. Fuck – I dunno the story. But there's summat on tonight. Half midnight. Down Trafford Park.'

'She tell yer this?'

'Who?'

'Cemetery bird. Good arse. The one needin a suntan.'

'Thought you were a leg man, Glassbrook?'

'In the thick of it now, aren't we, laddie?' He was about to say something else when Sandy put a brew and a butty down in front of me and another one down for him. He folded his arms, sat back in his chair, grinning at her.

'Owt else, love?' Sandy said.

'No, ta.'

Sandy left. Glassbrook whispered: 'They're fussy bastards. We can't even get fixed addresses. Whatever they're up to, this lot dint want the limelight that doin it in the capital would bring um.'

'Or the competition,' I said.

'Wunt make a bad copper, you.'

'Fuck off.'

'The cogs are turnin, laddie. Ever so slowly. You're probly our ticket to speedin this shite up.'

'This fun to you, ay? I've knocked your bloody teeth out n you're fuckin buzzin off it.'

He tucked into his butty, nodding as he scoffed it down. 'Not bad. Nice n soft.'

'Barmy. Everyone this week's barmy.'

'You aren't? What you doin this for again? Never told us.'

'Doin what? What am I doin? There's fuck all in this for us.'

'That's not—'

'I could finish the job with you – get round to that Ivey and do him a favour then be on me way.'

'Talk daft. No yer won't.'

'What?'

He swallowed. 'Cos you, deep down, enry Bane, are a sound bloke.'

One of the old-timers playing dominoes shouted: 'Blank. Bloody blank. No pips.'

'Let's get the bastards,' Glassbrook said to me.

I started on my grub, working fast – Glassbrook was pacing himself, his eyes kept watering when he got a twinge in his gums. 'They've probably been at it with Muhsi n that Safir for months,' I said, 'butterin um up. Must o been bringin them birds in for a bit, n all.'

'I bet they dint bank on the Paddys levellin a shitty shoppin centre.'

'Yeah,' I said. 'What a fuckin nuisance.'

'Was, wanit?' He laughed, filled his gob with more bacon bap before gabbing some more: 'Um – um – the see wi don nugosheeade wi teworists?' Gulped. 'We'll bloody negotiate with terrorists now—'

'How come?'

'Insurance, laddie. Think o the payouts. Big business involved. That's the sting. That's what's packin the wallop. First Canary Warf in Feb? Fuck you ceasefire. Now wiv ad this. Now us? Too many private-sector pennies wasted not to get this shite sorted fer good.'

'You were on the Manny case?'

'Aye.'

'Cock-up already?'

'I were reassigned.'

'You pull a sickie the day they made you all sign the Official Secrets Act?'

'You're one of us now, laddie. No secrets between us.'

I put the bag of crisps in my Harrington.

'Yer want um?' he said.

'Thought you couldn't eat crisps?'

'I can't. Be pushin salt in me wounds. The gnashers couldn't tek it.'

'You sure you're a copper, Glassbrook?' I said, still keeping my voice down. Then I stood up and said louder: 'Got a feelin you might've escaped from somewhere?'

'The zoo,' Sandy said, moving in to clear our plates.

26
PITSTOP

LATER ON. THE safe flat.

One bag missing.

The one I'd taken along to The Florencia. The one Emil had used on his own lab staff. On me and our Gordon. But the rest of the shooters were all there where I'd left them.

I unzipped a sports bag, chucked in the little CZ 99, a note with the Doll Princess's number on it in my handwriting, an MP5 and then zipped it back up.

Two missing.

There were a few beauties I'd taken out of the photo album and arranged a treat on the bedspread. The shaggers: Safir, Emil, the Doll Princess – at it like the bunnics down at Southern Cem.

I took out the mobile and dialled the last received call, pacing round the flat with it to my ear while it rang, wondering what to do with the place. I'd poured petrol into the other bags with our Maz's supply, soaked the rest of the big shooters, tried to wash away my prints – lobbed the canister about the flat until it was empty.

Torch it or turn it in?

. . . RING . . . RING . . .

Nobody answered but I dialled it again. At least this way I could gauge Glassbrook's reach. Test the loony. See if the bobbies danced when he whistled. He'd shown me a proper badge at the caff – MI5 papers, NCIS ID. A nutter like him in charge of the war? I wasn't that surprised.

'Glassbrook.' He even whistled his own name.

'It's me,' I said.

We had another chat.

The photos on the bed were petrol-wet – the burundanga brick on the pillow and all.

I still had the pimp's Zippo in my Harrington pocket and I took it out, picked up the bag I was taking – Craig Pendergrass's camera case in the same hand – and headed for the door.

Five minutes later and I was washing up by the motor with a bottle of Buxton and a mucky dash cloth, a good few side streets away from the safe flat. The bag was in the boot, sirens closing in.

27

FRUITS IN PLENTEOUSNESS ABOUND

11.20 P.M. DOWN Chester Road onto Pomona Strand. These were out-of-commission docks. Not quite Trafford. Not Salford. Not even Manchester. A dead space no-man's-land – half-a-mile's worth of abandoned canal tunnel under it.

I parked up off-road on a grass bank by the water, kept the lights off and the windows half-open. Stray cats were mooching about – this fly-tipped wasteland, all shitty derelict warehouses that wanted bringing down. A few empty offices were further back from the canal, but mostly it was scrapped construction. Industrial leftovers. Redevelopment began upriver, starting September, 2096.

A corner of Trafford Park was rusting over the water

– one or two floodlights still on over the junkyards behind the barbed-wire fence. That was it. No stars out. It was dark-dark round these parts. At least it was a blessing for cover but Pendergrass's camera wasn't exactly night-vision goggles. The city centre was quiet behind me. I opened the window a touch more. It was daft weather for this time of night – muggy, hard to breathe, hard to think, I felt it under my nails. The dead canal made it worse. The radio weatherman had said we might be on for some rain.

I tossed an empty packet of Golden Wonder onto the dash. Cheese and onion.

After a quarter hour spent listening to the strays scrapping and having it off, some van lights winked at me from across the drink. Another van pulled up next to it. I was on the wrong fucking side. With the extra light, I could make them out clear enough through the viewfinder. A couple of heavies got out of the front of the first van – shifty-looking lads, the sort that wore balaclavas to work. They signalled the boys in the other van and they all went round the back to open up shop. The party was starting early.

Click. Click.

A small motor pulled up next, followed by a black Transit van. *The* black Transit van, it was and all. Hallefuckinglujah.

Click. Click.

I looked at the time again.

Five to.

Still no sign of dibble.

I looked through the camera.

Emil was over there – dragging birds out of the vans, giving the fellers orders with just a nod, sorting out what was what.

Click.

He didn't look like he was nursing any war wounds from yesterday. I took my bad hand away from the camera lens and shook out the cramp. I thought of our Gordon. He was the one that had got the left arm full of lead.

Puncture holes everywhere.

Dots appearing fast on the canal surface.

Rain.

I stuck my own arm out of the window – let it pool in my hand. The rain was hot, getting heavier, smacking the hard mud now, kicking up on my windshield and bonnet. But I left the wipers off.

I dried my wet hand on my jacket and held up the camera – hanging half-out the window to get a better view across the canal. One of the heavies opened a brolly and kept Emil under it. Then Emil disappeared and so did the black van. Another quickly replaced it. Dolls changed hands.

When the pigs arrived I nearly sounded the horn, drumming Biggie's 'Juicy' on my steering wheel. 'Fuckin get in!'

It was all quick and easy. They blocked them with the Pandas and ARVs – lightbars swinging round and round but no sirens. No gobshite on some foghorn up in a helicopter, but you can't have it all like the pictures.

They must have pinched Emil first when he got off.

A roadblock round Trafford Park and it'd be job done.

I thought of my old man. The two of us watching Crazy Cagney in *White Heat*, Cagney getting his arse set up – pigs tailing him with all that fancy modern kit – the film was like some warning from the FBI. Unlucky sod, Cody. The bugger had a mole. *A copper? A copper?* Gutted.

I heard the spike strip working – tyres popped, hissed. They were like toy cars over there, spinning about in the wet.

Glassbrook and Ivey had shown up. Both of them. They were poncing about alongside the armed unit in full garb, getting pissed on. Just goes to show.

I rolled the windows up, wipers going mad, ready to head south, join the road again and stay clear of town.

The rain was a yellow sheet under the lampposts, pinging off the bent '50 Limit' sign. No slant. Fogged windscreen – I scrubbed it with my cuff and saw nothing but water and a wide empty road. I took the handbrake off – wheel spin, slick tarmac – I pulled out onto the lane, rev counter dancing in the red.

Then something came at me side on.

No headlights, no warning, everything juddered – worse when I skinned the crash barrier and turned. The steering wheel raced round. I knocked the side of my head on the door window. Cold air on my neck. The noise was just unreal.

The barrier finished and the motor span again and went over once. Turf at the top, sky at the bottom. The windshield made itself into a million little white squares.

An explosion threw me back in the seat. The car righted itself – went over again – then finished off tyres down.

Totalled and just back from the fucking garage. Absolute bloody bollocks.

I heard myself cough and felt it in my chest, out of sync with the sound. Things disappeared.

When I opened my eyes there was glass and water everywhere – on me, the dash, the passenger seat. The crash had turned the radio on. 'A Girl Like You' fuzzed in and out through the shot speakers – aerial somewhere down the road.

'Never . . . Never . . . Never . . .'

I was trapped in by the airbag, getting soaked through the empty sunroof. I tried the doorhandle. Buggered. The cockpit was all bent, mangled roof scraping my head.

And the rain.

My chin was wet with something else. Something black dribbling down me. I licked my lip. Just a gash. Nothing. Lips always bleed like mad.

There was a clang of metal on metal and somebody crowbarred the driver door open. The door squealed, bent outward, the glass in it was gone as well, and the whole car rocked when the hinges came off. Next, they slashed the airbag, and my legs came out of the footwell. They seemed to be dragging me for ages. A pair of strong hands – could've been two. I smelled the muck and wet grass outside. It was still throwing it down, loud as anything. They laid me out flat – my back sinking down in mud, gob open, hot rain on my tongue until I choked. When I coughed up the water, the Golden Wonders came up with it. Then a shape blocked the rain, put hands under my arms and started lugging me back again. Nothing worked. My arse went through the mud.

Eyes – half-open, wide open, half-open – shut. Shut for good.

28

AND POOR BIRDS MAY NOT BE FORGOT

I STOOD UP, coughing cold water. Eyes open but I was blind. There was water past my knees, I could hear it splash, feel it when I tried to move. I tipped my head to the side and smacked the water out of my ear – pressed a nostril down with a finger and cleared it. I swore and listened to myself echo. Everything to my waist was heavy and soaked – Glassbrook's mobile wasn't waterproof – but my top half was drier. I remembered the Zippo, had a feel around for it inside my Harrington and got it working.

Light.

I was underground. This tunnel made of rust and brick – high enough to stand up in and about three Gordons wide. The tunnel curved slow-right. I turned around twice and it was the same each way. A canal chamber. Dank and drippy like a sewer, stinking of rat piss. Bars of orange dripstone spiked the walls – made it look like a dragon's cave, great big rivets running down both sides of the brickwork. I gozzed phlegm into the black water and watched it bob.

Getting through was tough enough, there was allsorts in there. The water sloshed. The flame bounced on it, hurt my eyes.

Then my shin hit something big – it moved away and then the water rocked it back.

I took a grab with my free hand and was feeling up some wet clothes on a wide back, a mess of long straggly hair. I turned the whole lot over, kept my lighter above the splashing, wiped the guck and hair away from the face.

Abul Muhsi's body – swollen in the water.

I'd made a right mess of all this.

I left him alone, waded on for a minute and found myself on a long straight. I stopped trekking through the sludge when I heard the water moving up ahead – maybe some sod moving through it. There was loud breathing, spluttering like an old carburettor but I was sure it was my own.

Darkness.

The Zippo went out. I snatched the wheel, made another flame.

Light.

Somebody else lit theirs. Up ahead: a feller in a black balaclava. He ripped it off and dropped it in the water.

Emil's face glowed white in the tunnel. He held his lighter up and a circle throbbed around his hand.

He came at me, full speed – noisy – slowed by the water. I wanted to do one but I was too shaky. I let the Zippo die just before he swung his fist.

Nothing landed.

There was just a whoosh of air and then I wanted to sneeze.

Emil laughed in the dark – I could hear him slapping his hands together.

I breathed it in – a powder – coughed it out again, tried to – it felt like a lightning bolt in my brain.

My face went hot, everything itched, but the focus was on keeping hold of that Zippo – telling myself if I let it drop it'd be game over.

Other voices – out in front, behind me – foreign or Queen's English, I was clueless – too much echo.

Emil had his lads down here with him, playing lookout. I was fucked before. More fucked now.

My heart was loud, slowing down, still slowing. Hot blood – washing round me, stopping, hanging about for the next beat.

Have you sold my guns?

Laughing: 'Get fucked.'

Where did you take them?

'Cash Converters.'

Do they have them? Police.

'"Please?"'

He walloped me.

Police. Policemen.

Gozzing blood: 'No,' I said. 'No chance. Not the good stuff.'

Where?

'Don't ask me, mate. I'm seein unicorns.' I kicked him in the bollocks and ran. Then his hand on the back of my neck – my face in wall, water, wall again.

Laughter – not mine.

Somebody barked in English: 'TIME.'

Emil dropped me. Either he left or I left – hard to tell which.

I was out of breath and there was no Emil. No laughter. Nobody there.

The Zippo still worked – it had a blue flame now, wide and flat like a top grill on a gas cooker. I waved my hand around and the flame's ghost took too long to follow it. It stayed there, burnt on my sight.

I closed the lighter to wash my face – skin shredded loose, gasping at the cold, not the pain, shoving water up my nose to kill the itch. But it was too late. This was burundanga. I was already well on my way.

'You need to get out,' a voice said. Young. No accent.

Still nobody there.

'Give us a fuckin minute,' I said.

'You need to hurry up.'

'Which way then?'

'This way.'

My arm against soapy brickwork. I helped myself along. I listened for someone else. I couldn't concentrate hard enough.

Less water after a couple of minutes – still shin-deep.

Then things opened out and the tunnel split off into two.

'Left.'

I flicked the Zippo again. It was a giant blue sparkler, like the kiddies have on Bonfire Night, just bigger. I ran my fingers over the sparks, grabbed a handful – felt the heat but no pain. It was bright and gorgeous and it wasn't stinging my eyes.

'Left.'

'Alright, calm it,' I said. 'I'm goin.'

Sparks spat all over the place. They hit the tunnel roof and dropped in the water. The roof got closer, the tunnel got smaller.

I stopped and said: 'Oi?'

'Yeah?'

'You down here?'

'No.'

'So what, then? I've lost the plot. Gone barmy.'

Nothing.

'Still with us?'

'Yeah,' he said.

'Oi, where are you?'

'Here.'

I stopped and moved the sparkler to the right and there he was: Maggie the Witch's boy. Just a young lad, short for his age, bone-dry, blank-faced, wearing the same gear I'd last seen him in.

'How did you know?' he said, but his lips didn't move in time with the words.

'Just did. Clever bugger, me.'

'I'm showing you the way.'

'You're showin us up,' I said.

'I'm not here.'

'I've lost me marbles but nice one for comin. Like my little helper, you. Always there when I'm in a right pickle.'

'You're dead,' he said.

'You're fuckin dead, mate. I'm not fuckin dead.'

'You're dead,' Jacob said.

'Am I?'

'Yeah.'

'How is it you're helpin us, then?'

Jacob looked me up and down for a second. 'Were you ready to die?'

'Biggie is. I'm not.'

'Then you need to get out now.'

'Can't let um see us like this. Need to sort me head out first.' I was thinking aloud or maybe I wasn't.

Jacob reached out and took my free hand – little fingers smoothing down my palm.

'Gypos teach you this one, Jake?' I said, watching him trace the lines.

'Look,' he said. 'See. No lifeline.'

'Leave it out, yeah? Not that one again.'

'Dead.'

'Here we go.'

'Not you.'

'Who? Who's dead?'

'Her.'

I said: 'Bloody hell, son. Who?'

'Alice!' Jacob said but with my voice.

I snatched my hand back, spooked.

'Enry?' she said. No echo.

Christ.

We both turned our heads to the sound of my name. Jacob tried to take my hand again but I wouldn't let him.

'Enry?' She called out to me, sweeter than anything. That voice – not a day older than sixteen.

I was climbing the walls. 'Alice?' I said. 'Alice, love!'

'She's there. Why don't you go back to her?' Jacob said.

'Are you daft? She's gone, lad. I can't. Not goin back.'

'But you have gone back.'

'Don't fancy fishin stuff out o there,' I said.

'Plenty of fish . . .'

'Too right,' I said. 'I'm off.'

'Then go,' he said.

'Now?'

'She's here for you.'

I heard her footsteps sloshing towards us round the corner.

'Are yer there, love?' Alice said.

'I'm sorry, love,' I said.

'Can't leave us ere, enry. On me bill.'

'I'm sorry.'

'Comin mine fer tea? Mam's not in.'

'Is she not?'

'No.'

'. . . Right.'

'Well?'

'Can't, love.'

'Ow come?'

'Just can't.'

'Don't yer love us? Enry?'

I kept it shut.

'Come ere,' she said. 'Jus let us see yer fer Godsake.'

'No,' I said, filling up at the sound of her voice, feet trudging through the water louder.

Jacob tapped me.

'Go now,' he said. 'It's late.'

'Time is it?' I said, nodding at him for no reason.

'Time to go or time to ask her.'

'You're a proper rum one, Jake. Bet you're king o the playground, you. Runnin circles round um.'

'Too late,' he said.

I sniffed, wiped the tears out of my eyes. 'Does teacher call you Damien?'

'Enry,' she said, louder.

I turned my head and saw her, five feet away . . . four. She was just how I remembered her. In her school uniform. Hair dark, dead short, brave – some of the birds took the piss, called her a lad – but how could you say she looked like a lad with those tits? Decent tits, no need for any tissues stuffed in her bra like Jan or Sharon or the rest of the sweet-sixteen Poundswick birds. She had her school skirt rolled up, no tights on, no make-up, a jumper hiding her baby bump.

'What we doin then?' she said to me.

It was just me and her. Jacob had gone.

'Are you havin it?' I said.

'Yer don't love us,' she said.

'Oh, fuck off. I do. I fuckin said I do.'

'Ah love *you*.'

'Well then,' I said. 'Have it.'

'No.'

'Fucksake, Alice. Me n you, this is.'

'Am sorry,' she said. It was her turn to say it back to me.

Her belly shrank.

'Why didn't you have it?' I said.

'Ah dint av it cos—'

'Because what? Your mam know?'

'She took us, dint she?'

'Bet she fuckin did.' I was squinting down the tunnel, crying my bloody eyes out. I couldn't look at her. 'Well now you're dead, love – aren't you? So that's that.'

'We was jus kids,' Alice said.

'Yeah, I know.'

'N yer dad never liked us.'

'He did. Big fan, he was. Was up for bein a granddad.'

'Ee wan't.'

'Was. Never minded you stoppin round. Liked pervin on me birds.'

'Birds?'

'*Bird.*'

'Ah miss yer,' she said.

'I miss you. How did you ever end up on the game?'

'Enry?'

'Yeah, love?'

'Member us, yeah?'

'Course.'

I moved in to touch her but then she started wailing and I jumped back. She was thrashing about, blood all down her white legs. I screamed like a Mary. Alice was louder. I chucked the sparkler and was back in the dark, slapping my head, trying to claw her voice out of my ears. Sound stopped. My throat was fire.

There were scratches of light up ahead and I turned and ran down the tunnel – easier now, just like splashing through a mucky puddle, though I slipped on my arse twice.

My heart rate was still taking the piss:

Boom. Ages. Boom. Ages.

Only then I was climbing up.

Outside.

A white brighter than I could take. Then nothing.

Awake. A rush of motorway far far off – cars whipping past nonstop. I was in a soggy field somewhere on the bank of the Irwell – the sky darkish, clouds but no rain. I looked around for Jacob, Alice, Emil, anyone – wondering if la-la land was still open for business. I'd done my shoulder in and my left hand looked like purple glass – bubbly and giant with burns. The wrist was fucked. Maybe broken. Everything else ached.

By the time I'd tottered up to the motorway, some

of the headlights were coming on. A roar of Eddie Stobart trucks passed me and the wind dried my clothes off. It was getting on for night. I'd lost a whole day.

29

FAVOURS PART 2

I FOUND A phonebox. The glass was gone and so was the phone. I followed the road, kept to the grass and the dark – nobody beeped their horn. An Eccles estate started. Tower blocks. Station signs. Another phonebox.

Our Maz brought me a change of clothes. He turned up driving somebody's four-door Nissan. A gold paint job, custom spoilers, tunes on loud.

He opened the backdoor and there was a Blackpool beach towel on the seat.

'Bleed away. Ah knew yud get battered.'

'Nice one. New motor?' I said, getting in the back.

'Cousin's,' he said, turning the stereo down. 'What's that on yer fuckin and?'

'That is my fuckin hand.'

I took the Harrington off, carefully, wincing like a

mardarse. Next went the shirt – bloodstains thinned by the canal water.

'Lookin good, mate,' Maz said. He twisted round to get a decent view, resting a Christmas turkey of a forearm on the passenger headrest. He smiled, shook his head.

I said: 'How is it?'

'Death's doin better, mate. Sprised if yer dint get pneumonia. But that eye's on the mend – got a shiner worse on uva one now.'

I looked down: my ribs were yellow, black-and-blue. I was grazed up, slashed up, skin hanging, scabbing, weeping. 'Oi, you don't sound too concerned for us.'

Driving: 'Am ere, mate. Am jus fucked off yer dint ask fer elp.'

'I'm askin now.'

'Too late. Look at state o yer.' Maz took a hand off the wheel and fished around the glovebox. 'Ee-ah.'

He swung a Poundstretcher shopping bag at me. Inside it: fat square plasters, rolls of bandages, sticky tape. If a jacked Cortina fell on some unlucky lad in the pit, there was enough gear here to put them right. I said ta.

Maz said: 'Yer need to rest up, mate. Get that lot seen to. Yer wanna be in bed wiv ot water bottle n a brew.'

'Your sis fancy bein my hot water bottle?'

Maz put his foot down and the music got louder. 'Who's this?' I said.

'Ay?'

'This Nasty Nas?'

Maz turned it back down a notch. 'Jay-Z, mate.'

'Who?'

He nodded as he spoke: 'It's a – fuckin – whatsit. Yer know, Nas sample job, init?'

His sovereign tapped the gearstick. 'Piano's fuckin soft but drums are dead ard. Proper nice, init?'

'Best give us this.'

'Ee's feelin it, good man.' Maz eyed me in the rear-view, watching me dress my purple hand. I was impressed with myself. Maz went: 'Be cryin yer eyes out now, if it wan't fer us.'

I ignored him, concentrating. The road was smooth. 'Still not mard, are yer?' he said.

The little bandage roll finished in time with the tune.

'We got any Mobb Deep up there?' I said.

'Oo?'

'Any Biggie?'

'Might be able to sort us out some Biggie.'

Maz rattled a cassette out of the dash-pocket and fed the player.

Lights on in the dark, engine running. I left our Maz in the courtyard and shut the door with my foot. My hand was fat – gauze bandage – five mummy fingers meaning five minutes.

Otterburn Close.

Under the Kelzo walkway, along the ground-floor flats, past the trashed garages. Some of the drains were still flooded from last night – chucked club flyers turning to mush.

It was a bit too quiet. There were no gangs of kids knocking about, no Staffies barking, just a few pasty students heading home. A black feller with dreads was coming towards me in a donkey jacket, a Jamaican flag stitched on the chest, his arm round his white girlfriend. He was telling an Irish joke, fucking up the punchline, making her smile more. She finished it for him. Then she clocked me and lost the smile. 'See is face?' she said when my back was behind them. 'God.'

I walked up the right concrete stairwell, turned down the right deck and stopped at the right scratched door.

The Fold.

Nobody answered when I knocked. I waited a minute and then booted the door a few times but it wasn't opening. An ear to the wood: no music this time. Somebody was in, though – I could hear them moving around.

I went and leaned over the deck – looked down. There were lights on over the green, a young lad down there riding a girl's pushbike, another kid on a BMX doing wheelies alongside him.

'Jake!' I whistled with my good hand.

I knocked on the Fold again, still waiting for Jacob to come up when the door opened a split.

'Yer can't come in,' a weak voice inside – a bloke's – the door shutting again.

I kicked it wider and the bloke fell back, holding his face.

'You know the young lad what lives here?'

He shook his head, terrified.

'Then what you doin here?' I came in and shut the door.

He gulped. He was about twenty. Brown hair, bad acne, white Kappa hoodie with a stain down the front, baggy trackies, blue Reeboks.

'There's nowt ere, mate,' he said. 'Honest t'God. Av a look. Thev ad the lot. It's fuckin gone.'

'Who has?'

'Them lot out there. Everyone.'

The telly had disappeared, and the stereo. The budgie and all. Even its cage. There were dents in the carpet where furniture was missing, a paler patch of dirt where the sofa used to live – the one that I'd sat on with Gemma. A sleeping bag was on the floor instead of a coffee table. The posters and clippings on the walls, the tags – sprayed over each other half-a-dozen times still filled the gaff, made it look busy. But it was empty.

'Where's Maggie?' I said.

'The W-witch?'

Maybe the Fold had moved on to bigger and better things.

'Yeah,' I said. 'She nipped out for a loaf or what?'

'Through there.' He pointed to the kitchen – door shut, his arm shaking.

'Anyone else in?'

He said: 'No.'

I went for the kitchen.

'Wait,' he said.

'What?'

'Don't.'

'Just get off,' I said.

He nodded. I watched him roll up the sleeping bag, head out like a shot. When the front door shut I tried the kitchen.

The oxygen mask was on her face, blood inside where she'd coughed, hiding her gob. The tank was under the table, over on its side. She slump-sat in her chair, her neck hanging back over the backrest. It looked long, she was like a plucked goose strung up in a fancy butcher's. The rest of her was just potato skin.

Our Maggie had expired, just like the Fold.

I had a poke round the kitchen but there was nothing here. The cupboards were open, cleaned out, empty coffee pots on the worktop, no gear, everything robbed. Hard candle wax all over the table, broken flowerpots on the sill, the soil in the sink, not one baby mushroom – even a white empty space on the wall, shaped like a cross.

Where the fuck was it? Where would he put it?

I heard the front door, leaned out and saw Jacob in the front room, alone. He was wrapped up in a big blue Nike bomber – his face calm, empty. He had it with him in his hands, the sports holdall I'd given him to stash – it was bigger than he was. I thought of last night, tripping down in the tunnels under Pomona.

Jacob.

The real one was spooky enough.

'When did she go?' I said.

'Yesterday.'

I nodded to the bag. 'You stash it down in one o the garages?'

'Yeah.'

'No little accidents?'

Nothing.

'Give it us,' I said.

He came into the kitchen with the bag and lifted it into my good hand.

'You been kippin here?' I said.

'Yeah.'

'Your housemate left. Fuckin vultures, ay? Out there.'

I unzipped the main pocket and checked inside. Cold metal shooters.

Jacob went to take his bomber off, popping the poppers, not looking at dead Maggie once.

I said: 'Leave it on, mate. We're gunna go for a ride out.'

'Mate, five minutes my arse,' Maz said, back in the car.

I let Jacob get in the front with him. Jacob put his belt on, didn't make a peep.

'Av no booster seat,' Maz said to me.

'He'll be alright.'

Maz blinked across to Jacob – eyes back on me – then on the boy again: 'Alright, young man.'

'All right.'

'What team yer support, mate?'

No reply.

Maz said: 'Blues? Good lad.' Maz looked at me: 'Is mam know we're tekin im out on a school night?'

'Let's give her a ring,' I said.

Maz stroked his head, chubby fingers greasing through his hair gel. 'Serious?'

'Give us a mobile,' I said.

He passed me his phone and I took the note out the sports bag and dialled the number.

30

A GOOD HIDIN

'THEY'RE ON FIRE,' Jacob said, sat back in his seat, face tilted to the window.

Maz said to him, driving: 'Thema lights, them, mate. Jus the kebabies. Ah know some o these, me. Ungry?'

Jacob said: 'No.' We had a minute's silence and then: 'Are you?' he said.

'Yer what?'

'Hungry?'

'He's always after scran,' I said from the backseat. 'Check that chub.'

'Ay.' Maz slapped his belly. 'Birds, they go fer it. No need. "Ah love it when they call us Big Poppa."'

'Alright, Biggie.' I was laughing even though it hurt to. 'Oi, Jake, we can't let this one stop off for scran, can we mate?'

But Jacob's face was to the window again, blocking us out.

She was ten minutes late. I made Maz flash the lights and she flashed hers in the Kwik Save car park. She was driving the blacked-out bimmer. At least, I fucking hoped she was. I wanted to make sure nobody was with her. I had the sports holdall on my lap, in case she'd brought mates.

'Yer tekin that wiv?' Maz said, winding his window down as I dragged the bag out of the car.

'Aye.'

'Don't wanna know what's in it, do ah?'

'No, you don't, mate.'

'Nah, dint think so. Want us to follow yer?'

'Not with this lot.' I rattled the bag.

'Bane.' I ducked inside the open window, leaning on the door. His trout eyes were popping out, his cheeks flapping. 'Fuck's goin on ere?' he said.

I said: 'We'll have a catch-up, end o the week. Once this shit's over n I'm feelin meself.'

'Look, yer can kip at ours if yer need to, mate.'

'Might do. Cheers. We'll do that catch-up over a pint in the Red Beret. You havin that?'

'Yer don't drink.'

This time I got in the front and Jacob went round to get in the back. The seats were in nice nick – hard pale leather. The air-con was on low, the radio mute, cockpit-light glare.

I breathed in the clean perfume coming off her throat.

The dash clock said 23.13.

She looked small with worry, wide-eyed as I shut the passenger door. She was hunched up close to the big steering wheel, hair up – dry and fluffy, her neck seemed as slim as my wrist.

'You look terrible,' the Doll Princess said – lips open after the words had fallen out.

'I've seen you worse n all, love.'

She was in a thin dark top with push-up sleeves, black skirt, her legs were shaking – no tights on. Little boots for the pedals.

Jacob finally got in. She went for him, boots scuffing up the middle armrest as she scrambled over to the backseat.

I said: 'Easier to just get out, love.'

But she was tearing up: '. . . Jakob . . . Jakob . . .'

It was all too much – the emotional reunion. The lying cow. She held him. Tough little hands pressed her back.

She whispered something to him, I caught the odd foreign sound, muffled as she rubbed her face into his, covering his ears with her hands. He talked back to her in the same language.

I said: 'We drivin? I'd kill to have a go in this monster – only, I need a fuckin hand.'

She crawled back into her seat – arse first, swung her boots round into the footwell and fixed her skirt.

'You're welcome,' I said.

She kissed me – gob open – teeth nipping the cut on my bottom lip when she pulled away.

Her nose was pink. She smiled, keyed the ignition.

On the move.

I said to her: 'You knew he weren't dead.'

Her eyes flicked up to the rear-view. 'Yes.'

'Tellin us you didn't know where he was?'

'No. I didn't.'

If Emil had sold him to Maggie – what? – a year ago, that meant he'd been to Otterburn Close. He could've been the one that fly-tipped Safir's body there last week, dropped her into another warzone with plenty of suspects.

Emil and his boys had stashed their arsenal in that garage after a night visiting Formby, Gerry, Den and our Gemma. It was close by, convenient – the place was on his brain for a good few reasons.

Jacob had seen him.

'We goin back to yours?' I said.

She nodded.

'Where's that? In town?'

She was squeezing the steering wheel. Red knuckles, fists – whiter than white.

'You live with that Lance?' I said.

'He stays. Sometimes. Not tonight. He's busy. You've made him very busy.'

'Your own gaff? We have done alright, love, haven't we?'

'Do you hate me?'

'Why'd you lie to us? Tell us your kiddie was dead? You wanted him back. Isn't this why you dragged us into this? To get him. You must o known I'd twig it. Should o known I—'

'How?! How would I know these things?' She got upset and the accent finally came through. 'How?!'

But she couldn't have known. She didn't know about Otterburn Close, about Maggie and the Fold and what had happened to her Jacob. So why me? Why anything?

'It was safer for him,' she said, taking a hand off the wheel to scrub her face. 'To be forgotten. Not to see any of this. But I would have found him.' Her head turned – eyes off the road and on me, she pointed at her chest. 'I would have found him.'

We took the diversion, skipping the bombed-out streets to join Deansgate. She drove past what was left of the Kitchen Club. Hers was another swanky job. She drove into an underground car park below the building and the three of us got out and in to a shiny lift without a word. She pushed the top button and grabbed Jacob's hand. He was probably dying to read her palm.

Up we went.

The view out the glass window wall was making me queasy. As we got higher, I could see a corner of the city: town was wide awake. All those lights blinking around a quarter-mile of nothing.

Boom.

Kendals was still looking a bit sorry for itself.

Boom.

The CIS Tower battered and lonely.

Boom.

No Marks & Sparks.

We'd needed this bomb. They'd done us a fucking favour.

'That was on fire,' Jacob said. He pointed out the window and then smiled up at the Doll Princess and she cried again. The lift opened on a middle floor but nobody was there. I looked back outside.

The bomb was still in my head.

I plonked the bag on the glossy lift floor – the dirty silver tiles spinning like a flat disco ball – and then I tore my eyes away from the window. 'I don't do heights.'

Jacob took my good hand. Small, damp fingers – the skin was hard for his age. I remembered him holding that dead fox up by the throat, guts hanging out, sawing the head off with a Stanley knife.

I said: 'What are me chances, mate?'

The lift pinged open and she shooed him out.

'Saved by the bloody bell.' I picked the bag up and followed them down a red-carpet corridor.

Key in the door.

We'd got in before the rain started again, it was tapping a shut balcony window like it wanted letting in. I could see enough of the view from where I was standing to know it cost a fucking fortune.

Something cold touched my face. 'What is wrong?'

the Doll Princess said gently, stroking my cheek, fingers like ice.

'Tired,' I said. 'Just tired, love.'

The place was clean and tidy. No clutter. A posh open-plan flat – massive kitchen – silver breakfast table, two sinks, one of those big Yank fridges.

'Must cost a bit,' I said. It wasn't exactly Hulme Crescents. 'You've fell on your feet, Jake. This'll do for now, ay?'

He kept it shut, watching her watching me. She dropped her flat keys on the worktop, fixed Jacob a glass of water and took us into a bedroom. It was another big room: mirror wardrobe, a long beauty table, a futon couch next to the bed, a small table with a house plant on the other side. There were four walls and no window.

She wiped the back of her skirt tight and sat on the end of the bed, her legs together, not folded. Jacob stood with me, looking around, holding his water.

'Now you want to know what happened that night,' she said to me.

I bottled it, wasn't ready.

'So, you doin a runner, or what?' I said.

Of course she was.

'You gunna go home?' I said.

'No,' she said, 'I don't know.'

She was lying.

I coughed and felt it stab me inside.

Jacob sipped his water, turning the plant round on

the bedside table like he was checking the leaves. 'Jakob,' she said. He poured the rest of the water into the pot, left the empty glass next to it and came back over. He was holding a finger up to his mouth.

'What?' she said.

The front door rattled, opened, slammed shut.

'Shit.'

We heard two fellers gabbing but there could've been more. One of them called out a name.

She pushed us both in the mirror wardrobe, kissed Jacob's forehead before closing the doors to. The mirror doors were a window on this side, the light from the room came through enough to see. It was a proper walk-in wardrobe, behind me: two-dozen pairs of Bally and Ferragamo shoes – lined up in rows, smelling of polish, a duty-free job. There were skimpy frocks on the rails and plenty of room for next season.

A decent-sized video camera was on a tripod aimed at the glass doors.

We watched Lance come in the bedroom. Silver temples, blue suit, brown holiday tan. The Doll Princess stood by the sofa with her arms crossed, her weight on one leg as he pecked her cheek but didn't touch her. He had gloves on. Emil came in next holding a black suitcase which he lobbed onto the bed, watching it bounce.

'We're all going tonight,' Lance went. He sounded well-to-do. He wasn't a Brit.

The suitcase was settling on the duvet. She'd have to be ruthless.

I turned the video camera on – no tape in it.

Jacob was behind me, straightening the rows of shoes.

I felt the clothes, making sure the hangers didn't squeak on the rail – checked the pockets, cuffs, anything. I tried the shoes, reached inside all of them – had a feel around the toes. Tipping them would make too much noise, could give us away.

It was in a riding boot at the back.

COPY.

I pushed the little cassette in the camera and it asked me to record or press play. I hit rewind with a bandaged finger, stopped, twisted the view screen up so I could see it properly and kept it from the lad.

Turning round, I saw Jacob with his eyes on me like something out of *Village of the Damned*.

We'll be alright, I mouthed, nodding down at the bag.

He knelt and started to unzip the main pocket for me, slowly, so as not to make a sound.

I spun down the volume wheel and pushed play. The tape was jumpy for a second and then we had Abul Muhsi's hairy arse going back and forth. He was stood over the futon, giving a young white lad a seeing to. Gerry.

The bedspread was a different colour but the room was the same as how it looked out there now. The two of them shifted positions and Gerry dropped half out of shot.

Out there: Lance was giving the Doll Princess a hard time. He asked her why she'd needed the car. She did her best to keep them from starting the packing. Hearing her talk to Lance was odd. She was cold – never the smiler – lying through her teeth and doing a grand job. She stormed out the bedroom, said it was to get a drink but really to get them to shift. Lance followed her out, talking, talking. Emil stood there, looked across at his reflection – looked right at me. He rubbed the back of his neck with his fingers, rolled his shoulder, and then he left too.

On the screen: Safir wandered into the room, gorgeous in a short red frock, tugging my Alice along by the wrist. Safir was trying out for the Pouty Bad Girl and was well on for getting the part. Her skin was like Ovaltine. That long black hair swishing as she looked back at Alice.

Alice stumbled in Gemma's tall heels – they didn't look right on her. Safir pulled her on the bed and arranged her on all fours, in profile for the camera. I squinted at the screen. They must've been working this shagathon into a regular thing – at Safir's place and here. Safir had a big pair of dressmaking scissors in one hand and she peeled Alice's frock up over her arse and then cut her out of it, a straight line up the back. Snip-snip. Frilly knickers and all. Kinky cow. Only Gemma's shoes stayed on.

Safir made Alice do a couple of lines of what must've been burundanga and then the Doll Princess came and sat in the chair at the beauty table. Maybe she was watching them but the camera only caught her legs. Alice was sitting up on the bed now, legs spreadeagle, Safir wanking her. My Alice was gone – this was a blank domino – no sodding pips. Shiny eyes, shiny gob – totally out of it.

Next up was Emil. He arrived with his kit off, standing at the side of the bed, swigging a bottle of clear spirit, watching those two go at it. He twisted round to the Doll Princess and grinned, the neck of the bottle in his fist.

The tattoos on his back squirmed as he dived in for a go on Safir. He switched to my Alice and finished inside her quick. Safir stretched a hand out for the Doll Princess and she stood up and took it, scooped her dress off and crawled onto the bed, tagging Emil out. Emil picked up the booze and left the room knocking it back, his cock half-mast in a johnny, swinging.

There'd been six of them. Now five. The place was still too crowded. Muhsi finished next, belting his big suit pants up before he fucked off, probably to find the bathroom, taking that Gerry with him for round two.

Now it was just the three. Ladies' night. The birds left to it.

The Doll Princess kissed Safir, who pulled away to kiss Alice. She licked Alice's face, slowly from chin to cheek to temple, like it was a drippy 99. Alice didn't move, didn't blink. I watched Safir laugh on mute. They were all on one.

Next, Safir took the big scissors and, snipping the air, managed to cut Alice with them. An accident. It looked like she'd caught a finger, or maybe the whole hand. But the blood charmed her. Next thing, Safir was poking Alice's tits, trying to snip at her nipples – sticking the blades in and then shaking them into her belly. The Doll Princess wrestled Safir for the scissors and won, both of them thrashing around over Alice's body.

I wiped my tears away and kept watching.

She hammered the scissors, blades together, into Safir's throat. The third stab was the winner. The blood jetted out across the bed, a good few arcs before the fountain dried.

Alice's body stopped twitching. Safir's stopped too – she was on her back, her head hanging over the edge of the bed, crossways, eyes open and straight into the camera. The slits in her neck were gaping like extra mouths.

The three of them were covered in it. Cream Egyptian cotton bedsheets turned red on red.

Everybody came back in the room. Emil first and then Gerry and Muhsi. Gerry was quick, I'd give him that. He was right on the ball. Muhsi tried to leg it too but Emil made sure he didn't get far.

Everybody came back in the room. Out there.

I switched the video camera off. I swallowed, didn't sob.

Lance came towards the wardrobe. 'I'll help you start!' he shouted. The Doll Princess tried to stop him but Emil held her.

Jacob covered his ears. Smart lad.

I was crying for me, knowing I'd remember Alice this way – like this – till the day I fucking went. But I was crying for her too, and even that murdering cunt Safir, and for Jacob and his mam, and those two fuckers out there as I squeezed the trigger.

Lance took one somewhere in his middle. He did a funny pirouette, fell out of my line of sight and then Emil was shooting at me.

The rest of the glass came through and I dropped on my backside, still firing. More shaky flashes came from Emil, popping with a right bang, the noise blinding – like cherry bombs going off next to my ear.

'Let's fuckin have you!' I said, teeth together, under the racket. But the bullets stopped whizzing through the silencer. My finger had jumped out of the trigger guard and it all went quiet.

Shoes collecting empty cartridges.

Ears left with a buzz.

Then I heard the Doll Princess scream: 'JAKOB!' She was under the beauty table. Jacob ran out from behind me and she grabbed him by his blue bomber and took him down.

Emil had vanished. He was hiding somewhere else, not in the room.

I came out of the wardrobe. Lance was on the floor, messing up the carpet. I touched his arm and he flapped like a seagull.

His eyes rolled back to find me.

'Your world has just stopped.'

His mouth made the words but the sound wasn't quite there. I was going fucking deaf.

'Do it,' he said.

Do it. Do it.

Snuff him?

But I saw Emil nodding with a shooter, wrong side up in the broken bits of mirror on the floor and I fired at him. Emil slipped back round the door. I shot-up the bedroom wall for a second. A wavy line of crumbling white, plaster pumping out like flour. The clip ran out. The smoke went. I dropped a submachine gun and pulled a CZ 99 with my decent hand.

Out the bedroom: no sign of life. The front door of the flat was open. I did a tour of the rest of the gaff to make sure, took my time – bathroom, box room, front room – I even braved those balcony windows. Nothing. I went into the bedroom again to put the shooters back in the bag. Lance was gone, just a puddle of blood – the trail stopped before the carpet finished. I stuck my head out of the room and saw that the front door was shut.

Back in the bedroom: the Doll Princess was hugging Jacob on the bed, he didn't look too charmed but he wasn't in a state. That boy had problems.

'Emil,' I said to her. 'He came back in for Lance? Speak up. My ears.'

I lip-read the answer: I shouted but you didn't hear.

I said: 'I still owe him a good hidin.'

She said something else to me, rocking Jacob in her arms to comfort herself.

'Say again?' I watched her trembling gob.

Police? The pigs would be on their way.

'Some bugger'll be onto the cop shop by now,' I

said, flicking a finger inside my ear like it would turn the sound up. 'Jake, anythin you can do bout this, mate?' I knew he wasn't Jesus but, fuck me, it was worth a go.

31

HENRY

FRIDAY MORNING. IT felt like my first time out in the world. Half-ten and I was walking up the street in a black wool tie that belonged to my old man, black brogues – shiny with half a tin of Kiwi polish, a black suit – no Harrington. My face was still blacked-up too. I caught a glimpse in the window of a parked Vectra and lifted my shades. My eyes were getting better but still swollen, great big circles like a bloody racoon, just starting to fade.

It was a decent day for it. Lucky, since the weekend was supposed to be another washout. We had blue skies, birds singing, all of that.

My Alice in a box. It was done.

I passed the gates to Southern Cemetery, thinking. They didn't give every baby a funeral.

*   *   *

Manchester Crem. Our Jan was finishing a fag. She was stood on her own by the flowerbeds. She watched me as I came up the drive and stuck her hand up and waved. The hand went over her gob when I got closer.

'God!' she said. 'Bloody ell, lovey! Yuv bin through the wars, ant yer?' Her brow creased, eyes already wet without my doing, waterproof make-up holding strong.

'Bad do with a couple o fellers last week,' I said, putting my arms round her.

Jan's hair was done nice, a short salon job she'd combed back over her ears. She pressed her face up against my chest and said 'God . . . God . . .' until I let her go. 'They mug yer? Did they tek owt?'

She wore a short black top under a short black coat. Bursting pencil skirt. Pattern tights. White heels.

'They got the motor,' I said, 'but it's been taken care of.'

A frown: 'Bastards.' A grin: 'Want wurf messin wiv yer, was it?'

'Let's get in there, ay? Who's here?'

Our Jan took my good hand, squeezed it and gave me a look.

I said: 'What?'

'Wait n see.'

The coffin came in. I sat down on the back row but Jan made me get up again and sit with her nearer the front.

The turn-out was pretty slim. No one else from the Poundswick year came. Not even Sharon or any of the other birds we used to knock about with.

Alice's mam turned round with her nose in a hanky and said: 'Enry? Is that you wiv yer face out ere?'

'Ee were mugged,' Jan said for me.

'Iya, Mrs Willows,' I said.

Smiling: 'Used to call us Bev.'

'I am sorry, Bev.' I put an arm round Jan. 'You remember Jan, Bev? Same class as Alice.'

'Course ah do. Wiv said ello. Am glad to see some o Alice's friends. Thanks fer comin.' She blew her nose and cried.

Jan stood up and bent over the row to give her a hug. I did too.

The service still hadn't started and I thought they might be waiting a minute to see if a few more buggers would show but then the vicar told us to stand and they played 'Love Comes Quickly' – Pet Shop Boys.

Jan nudged me and mouthed: *Er mam wanted summat else. But this were er favourite.*

We had 'Bridge Over Troubled Water' at the end. A bit more traditional.

In between the tunes, the feller had stood behind the podium and said God said Justice said Hope said Forgiveness.

I'd turned round between Justice and Hope and seen my old man sat on the back row.

Alice Willows went behind the curtain and we all

stood up again and hung our heads. I told her I was sorry, over and over.

Jan was mad nobody had come out for Alice's funeral. I thought at first she was trying to be angry for Bev's sake but Bev wasn't mithered about it. We walked out with her, holding an arm each. Jan started giving her reasons: 'People dint know bout it, Bev. There's not bin nowt in the papers wiv all that to-do what wiv the Egypt girl. Jus that one tiny thing on Thursday. It's not bin bloody right.'

'Ah know, love,' Bev said outside, hugging her, looking at me.

'You been readin bout that then, Jan?' I was buttoning my jacket after a relative took Bev off our hands. 'Bout Safir Hassan?'

'Oh, aye. Thev found im. Yesterday. Bastard what did it.'

'Muhsi?'

'That's im,' Jan said. 'Dead.' Jan went quiet for a second, touched my tie and then let go and looked at her shoes. 'New these. Got um fer today,' she said. Eyes up. 'D'yer like um?'

'Nice.'

She waited for me to say something else but I didn't. 'Yer see im in there – at the back?' she said.

'Who? Me dad?'

'"Oo? Me dad?" *Yeah!*'

I said: 'He liked our Alice when I brought her round. He used to go "tek care of er. No one'll av a bad word t'say bout that one." N he should've been right.'

Jan turned round: 'Ee's ere now.'

He was chatting with Bev and two older fellers I hadn't met – but he had one eye on me. I nodded hello.

'I'll have a word in a bit,' I said to Jan and kissed her cheek.

She tried for a smile. 'Not off are yer? Comin pub, yeah? Enry?— Ah mean Bane.'

'Henry's alright, love. Yeah. Give us half-hour. Where's the do?'

'No do. Everyone's jus goin back to Wythie fer a bit. Cock o the North fer a few n then maybe—'

'Not the Red Beret?'

Jan showed me her teeth again. 'Could do, yeah. You alright fer gettin down? Wiv sorted a lift.'

Bev and one or two family started to get in the back of the funeral car.

'Don't worry, love,' I said. 'I'm comin.'

Jan nodded, gave me another squeeze and then caught up with the rest who were walking and talking. I watched her get out her fags, offer one to my old man – he said no thanks. Then she linked an arm through his and they turned down the drive to get out the gates, waving at Bev as the car went past. The whole gang left.

'Mr Bane.'

I turned round and nearly took Ivey for a pallbearer. He'd swapped to a black three-quarter-length mac. Square shoulders, arms behind his back, feet together – he looked like General Tosser, 1st Battalion. I walked over. His bugle was sideways.

'Missed us, mate?'

'This way,' Ivey said, without looking at me.

We started towards the van.

'Sorry bout the face,' I said.

He stared. 'I'm not sorry about yours.'

Own goal.

32

GONE

GLASSBROOK WAS BEHIND the wheel. He reached over, unlocked the squeaky door and I climbed in and shut it on Ivey and nearly had his fingers. His face was like a smacked arse.

Glassbrook laughed, pointed to his wrist and said: 'Five minutes.'

Ivey took a stroll.

'Soft touch some o these fairies,' I said.

'Tellin me, laddie. Specially the big buggers.'

'This van,' I said. 'Can't they sort you out with somethin a bit more glamorous?'

'Ay! I asked um fer this,' Glassbrook said.

'How's the gob?'

'Pain.'

'Think o the compo.'

'Ow was it?' he said.

'What? Funeral?'

'No, tekin that bruisin. Gutted I missed it.'

'It was a car crash. The funeral was alright,' I said. 'Did a good job in the end.'

'Good.'

'Yeah.'

'Made yer peace?'

There were sunglasses on the dash.

'You see the video?' I said.

'Not one fer "You Bin Framed". All fer a bit o sex n violence. Mad cow.'

Lance must've been about to blackmail Safir and her matron, that poor sod Muhsi.

Shaggin. Safir the sex monster. But that was the least of her problems. So that Lance got friendly with Terence Formby because his club was where Safir liked to spend her evenings. He convinced Formby to help set Safir up and in return, take a cut of the money. But Formby probably wanted to pull some of the weight himself. He got Lance to give him some of the snaps of Safir getting her arse shagged off – a promise of a copy of Tuesday night's porno still to come.

Only it didn't go to plan.

'They botched that right up, dint they?' Glassbrook said.

Terence tried to deny it, but he was pally with Gemma's pimp, Den. Terence gave him some of Emil's burundanga to hold, as a precaution, in case getting into bed with this Lance turned out to be a shit idea. Which it did.

Glassbrook looked at me. 'Yer know Safir – she might've been through a few Alices.'

I said: 'Never know now, will we?'

'We might,' he said.

'Papers still don't know what went on. No one in there, neither. Not even her mam.'

'It's delicate. Jus give us time, laddie.'

'This gunna be a whatsit? A cover-up?'

'Cover-up?' he said. 'Clear off. It's not fuckin "X-Files".'

I opened the glovebox. Empty Blue-Ribbon wrappers dropped out. I closed it back up in time to catch a Jaffa-Cake box. 'They both alright then, or what?'

'Er n the kiddie?' Glassbrook said. 'Wiv still got um. Fer now.'

Emil had sold the little lad to Maggie last year for some gear to keep his first batch of birds quiet. He must've had a taste for the herbal shit because it was cheaper than smack. Fuck knows, before they'd started making burundanga under The Florencia. Maybe it'd happened later, maybe Safir had turned him on to it, maybe he was just greenfingered. I thought about Jacob – how he'd only just found his mam again. I thought about fox blood, knives, garages, ghosts.

'Where do the shooters fit in?' I said.

'They were probly gunna shift um wiv the young ladies at the docks. There's always some thug bastards oo wanna get their ands on a gun. Decent kit fer a decent price. You'd know.'

'Would I?'

Two missing.

'Course, they must o bin andy when it come to cleanin up the fallout.'

Black Transit vans. Balaclava boys with heavy shooters.

'Bane, wiv got Nikolin.'

'Well in. Gunna hand him over to them lot in Holland for the trial? Thought they were sortin out the Balkan bastards.'

'You mean The Hague. Nikolin's a bloody soldier not a bloody general.'

'He's a bloody nutcase.'

'Lance Mora's still on the run. Could be gone by now.'

I said: 'Gone? As in abroad? Last I saw o Lance, he wasn't fit for his holidays.'

Flapping like a seagull.

I said: 'You gunna take care of us, Glassbrook?'

'Pends how yer mean.'

'Keep n eye out.'

'Stay out o trouble, laddie, n I might look out fer yer. Might keep yer posted on this lot. Now get out. It's back to the office fer us.'

'You mean, KFC.'

'Out.'

'I was hopin for a lift.'

'The cheeky get.'

I put my seatbelt on this time. 'Nice one,' I went.

Glassbrook shook his head, sighed, whistled. He

looked out the windshield. 'She were a piece o work, Safir, wan't she?'

Alice.

He started the van. 'Yeah, well. Gone now.'

33

ROUNDS

SPECIALS SCRAWLED UP the frosty glass.

'Dint know they did grub ere?' a punter said.

Another bloke pulled a face. 'Ah wunt say they do.'

'Owt else?' A patient barmaid said to me, watching me fish through my coins with a single hand. She was staring at my face, dying to ask: what happened, love?

I came from the bar with a bag of crisps in my gob, carrying two drinks in my arms, one hand in bandages, still out of action.

'Mission Impossible,' one feller said as I made it to the booth without spilling a drop.

I said to our Jan: 'Here's your next, love. Bev, want another?'

'No ta, love,' I heard Bev shout from the next booth.

Jan said: 'Oh ta enry. Should o said yer was ere – would o elped yer.'

I sat down, made out that I was mad. 'I managed.'

'Lovey!'

'I'm just kiddin.'

I spoke to Bev later on. She'd moved to Nottingham three years ago to be with some feller but it hadn't worked out and she'd planned on coming back home in September. She hadn't heard a peep from Alice since Christmas 94. Must've been some bust-up.

Someone let my old man out of the next booth and he came over and shuffled opposite me and Jan, a black Harrington under his arm.

He was wearing a clean shirt that he'd had a go at tucking in and a too-short wool tie with the little knot pulled down from the neck. Still a scruffy get.

Jan said: 'Iya, enry – jus nippin t'loo,' dibbing a butt in the ashtray.

My dad was Henry. I was Bane.

I let Jan out of the booth and she brushed my leg as she squeezed through, making sure I felt it.

We sat down and I took a sip of my drink. He picked his up too, the beer mat with it, stuck on the bottom of the glass.

Silence.

'What've yer got?' he said.

'Kaliber,' I said.

'Puffter.'

'Cheers.'

'Want anuva one?'

'I'm alright, Dad.'

Silence.

'Poor girl, ay?' Dad said.

'How'd you hear?'

'*Evenin News*. Rang um up. Give us runaround first but put us back in touch wiv Bev.' He took another gulp. 'N ere I am.'

Sixty-one and the old bugger had put a bit on round the waist but the rest of him looked thinner. His black hair was going white. His eyes were smaller than I remembered. He could've done with a shave.

'Still livin in town, then?' I said.

'Stockport at the minute.'

'Not far.'

'Yer workin, son?'

'Payin the bills,' I said. 'You?'

Dad nodded. 'Thas all yer want.'

Silence.

Then he said: 'Alice, she were n only child, like you. Look ow yer both turned out.'

'I'm not bloody dead.'

'Oi, get this one a mirror,' he said, throwing his hand up. 'Yer look near nuff dead to me, son.'

'It's been taken care of,' I said.

'Look, yer don't get a face like that fer nowt.'

'Where'd you say you were workin?'

He finished his pint and carried on. 'Or maybe yer do these days. Ah dunno.'

'Another one?' I said.

'Member yer mam?'

'No, Dad, can't say I do.'

'Smart arse. She were a miserable cow. Every day were a funeral to er. Know what did her?'

'The drink,' I said.

'No, son. It were us.'

'How many've you had?'

'Yer Alice – she were a good one. Grand, she were. What appened? Ow'd she end up in such a right mess?'

'Who knows?'

'Could've ad that one down the aisle. After yer finished wiv school. Ad some babies n bin on yer way by now.'

'Dad.'

'She were better than that lot yer were chasin fore n after.'

'She was,' I said, getting up with my jacket.

'Not eadin off?'

'Gents,' I said.

'Am sorry,' he went. 'Tek care, son.'

'I do.'

'Tek more care.'

'I'm stayin,' I said. 'Just goin to the gents.'

He frowned. Screwed his eyes up. 'Ay? That me tie?'

Jan was slotting quids into the cig machine by the toilets when I came out.

'Bastard,' she went.

'Need change, love?'

'Need summat.' Her face was up to the machine, hand slapping the side of the glass.

'How's your Trenton?' I said.

'Back in school. Thank fuckin God.' She bit her bottom lip and looked at me. 'Sorry.'

'Any joy with the job?'

'Got it. Shit, though. But it's money, init?'

'Get in, Jan. Well done, love.'

'Am not celebratin.'

'Could do.'

'Could *we*?'

'Yeah.'

'Tomorra night?' she said.

'Can do, yeah.' I kissed her neck and headed over to the jukebox.

. . . Whitesnake . . . The Who . . . Jackie Wilson . . . Stevie Wonder . . .

Back one to *The Very Best of Jackie Wilson*.

'No Pity (In The Naked City)'.

I bought a half and put it under my old man's nose and sat back in the booth opposite.

'Pace yourself,' I said.

'Goin casino after this,' he said. 'Fancy comin? Keepin old o money fer us?'

'Make sure you don't spend it in one go?'

'Aye, son.'

'Another day.'

The song came on. Wilson sang. 'Soppy bugger,' he said. 'Oo put this on? You?'

'Yeah.'

'Teks us back, this.'

I said: 'To when?'

34

THE START OF YOUR ENDING

MAZ WORKED UNTIL seven but he'd given me a key. He lived in one of those three-floor terraces off Platt Lane with a couple of his cousins, but they were both visiting the family abroad, due back in a month.

I put the key on the table in the hall. The multi-stack in the front room was turned up, Presley on the go.

'Little Sister' – the treble way too high.

'Maz?' The door was open, the room was empty.

It must've been a prank.

I killed the volume and took the CD out, sorted through the cassettes and put Mobb Deep's *The Infamous* on quietly. My copy.

On the kitchen fridge, there was a new note scribbled in Maz's big capitals:

BANE –

BACK BY 6. TAKEOUT MENUS ON THE SIDE. CHINESE?
– MAZ

We'd gone for Chinese last night. I touched the kettle.
Still warm. I opened the bread bin. There was a brick
of burundanga stuffed inside – paper-wrapped, the
corners folded up at the end – resealed.

I went back into the front room and turned the music
off and listened.

A toilet flushed – the pipework so upset it let the
whole house know. The downstairs bathroom was under
the landing, the door was shut, but unlocked. I opened
it towards me.

Maz was sat on the toilet lid in his work overalls –
duct-tape over his gob, feet together, tape round his
ankles, tape round his wrists. His elbow was still
pushing the toilet handle down. He tried to say something, stamped his feet as best he could.

I saw someone in the cabinet mirror, standing in the
hall behind me.

Maz's fish eyes were blinking. He was still umming
at me through the tape.

'Diggin the belt, Frank,' I said.

'Versace,' Frank said. 'They're back in.'

It was a snake belt, hooked round him tight – and it
didn't look thick enough to hold his gut in for long. He
was really dressed up for the occasion. A pastel polo shirt
with the collar up underneath a dark boxy jacket, loose
tonic pants – turned up twice, and white tennis shoes.

When I came out from the bathroom, two massive lads appeared behind Frank, blocking the front door.

Heavy feet on the stairs. I looked up and saw another big feller. He sat halfway down and watched. He was older, his chin in his palms, head the size of a watermelon.

I didn't know any of these lads and they didn't know me.

'Did yer preciate the Elvis?' Frank said.

'Nice touch,' I said.

'It's bin on fer an hour. Wiv ad a fuckin sing-along while we were waitin, ant we lads?'

'Bin fuckin quality,' said one of them next to Frank.

'Oh, aye,' the big feller on the stairs.

'Stoppin for a brew, Frank?' I said.

'Had one,' he said. 'We all have.'

'Course.'

Frank's hair was combed into a tidy Brylcreem block but the mutton chops were waxed down, in need of a trim. He laughed for a bit, face wobbling, holding his belly, and then said to me: 'Not bad this Paki's place. Convenient fer town. But there's a lot o dodgy gear in this gaff, Bane. Allsorts pinched. Drugs about. Guns. Not touched any o that bollocks, av yer? Be careful, son. Wunt wanna be found wiv me arse angin out around ere when the bobbies come knockin.'

'Frank—'

His face went still: 'Get im in that room.'

The two lads behind him came for me and took an arm each.

'Oi, watch the hand.' I shouldered one lad off into the wall and barged into the front room myself.

'Take a seat,' Frank said, the next one in, boys behind him again, the big bloke from the stairs shutting the door.

I sat on the far end of Maz's sofa.

'Glad yer turned that rap shite off.' Frank went to the stereo and flung the tape out.

Elvis was back in the building.

'I Beg of You'.

Frank sat next to me and put his big gloved hand on my knee. Pat. Pat.

The King talked the lyrics – out of time with the King. 'Yer know ah ate to cry . . . but that's what's bound to appen . . . if yer ever say goodbye.'

There was a time when we'd have these tunes on the go in the back of the Britton. Only when he was out. Just to take the piss.

Frank shut his eyes. He was dying to croon. 'Thought we'd leave yer to it, did yer, son?'

'Never know. Thought you might,' I said. 'I don't owe you any cash.'

'Now, now – yer took the piss, dint yer, Bane? Yer took advantage. Y'owe us more than cash.'

Pat. Pat.

'N yuv bin idin,' he said.

'Just restin up.'

'N that Paki in the bog's bin elpin yer out.'

'Leave our Maz,' I said. 'He's alright.'

'Ee's a City fan,' the big feller said, clocking Maz's dirty away shirt on the back of an armchair.

'Do yer know where the word thug comes from, Bane?' Frank said.

'Can't say I do.'

'The Pakis,' he went. 'See, the Thuggies were these Paki lads what lived donkeys ago. Bad buggers. They'd unt round place to place, lootin the travellers, thievin n killin. A band o Robin oods wivout the givin back. They used to do big ighway robberies n then execute on sight. Yud be frightened o comin across a Thug in them days, cos yer weren't gunna be meetin one twice. They were clever boys – spreadin fear like that. They ad everyone fuckin brickin it. The *fear*. Fuck me, imagine it? Them Pakis might as well of ad fuckin magic powers.'

Frank stopped talking and patted my knee again. 'Do yer think you're a thug, Bane?'

I kept it shut.

'Avin power over someone else. Mekin um shit scared o yer. That's ard graft. But avin real power over *yerself*. That's harder. That's slippery, son.' He was tapping his feet to the Elvis, shaking his right knee so much it was speeding his words up. 'Power's what meks a bloke feel tough.'

The King belted the last round of chorus out. Frank's tennis shoes were together on the carpet, going like windscreen wipers.

He smiled and said: 'Know what meks *us* feel tough?

It's not actin like a thug – al give it yer, it's a funny one – steppin out onto a busy road, the second after the car orns go – as them tyres screech, when the bird you're wiv squeezes your hand, calls out your name cos fer a second she thinks she's about to fuckin die.'

'Frank—' I tried again.

He pushed his glove back to see his Omega. 'That ten-to?' he said, holding the watch face up to his nose. 'Ah need specs.' Then all he had to do was look sideways at one of the new fellers and the multi-stack went off. The dopey lad had a root for the off switch but ended up having to unplug it. Elvis died twice and things went quiet.

But there was still one King left in the front room.

Frank said to me: 'Yer know, that Stark dropped us off a present, uva day.'

Stark? Trevor the Chemist's guard dog?

'New gear,' he said. 'All a bit fancy. Not my speed.'

He meant the brick I'd left at the lab.

Frank laughed again, looking round the room like he was showing me off to them: 'Look at that face,' he said. 'N the rest. The boy's got bruises on is bruises. Someone's already started us off. Be rude not to finish the job.' He stood up, leaving a crater in the sofa seat, and went: 'Lads.'

The big feller was up first. It would be like stopping a National Express with a butterfly net. No chance.

He struck out a long line of duct-tape off the roll, snapped it with his yellow teeth and I let him get on with the job. He was wearing leather gloves, the lot of them were – we used to get them for three-fifty, Arndale Market.

When he'd done my hands and feet, Frank bent down and squared up to my face. 'Av all kinds o friends, Bane.' Neither of us blinked. 'Some of um wear red. Some wear blue. They all think they're fuckin thugs.'

'We talkin footy?' I said, before my mouth met tape.

'We're talkin dibble,' one of Frank's boys said, stood at the window, twitching the net curtain.

Sirens outside.

From the sofa, I could see out the window – the blue lightbar flashing round on the Panda roof. The pigs had parked outside. Two of them got out, putting their daft hats on straight and heading up the front plot. We heard another siren. There were a few arriving.

Frank stood up and went: 'Out the back, boys,' and they all started to shift. Frank grinned. 'Ta-ra, Bane.' He mimed a guillotine to the neck with his hand.

I was alone for a minute.

Then: 'Bane! Bane!'

Maz.

Maz was loose. He ran in, snatched the tape off my gob, a steak knife working on my hands until he'd cut me free.

The doorbell went twice, then twice again, then the knocking started, then the ramrod.

The pigs had a warrant. Frank had planned the lot.

ACKNOWLEDGEMENTS

Cheers to: Andrew Cowan, Lavinia Greenlaw, Amit Chaudhuri, Trezza Azzopardi, Natasha Soobramanien, Jean McNeil, Mark Currie and Robert Clark; my classmates at UEA; Peter Straus and Sam Copeland of Rogers, Coleridge and White; Tom Avery and all the staff at Jonathan Cape; my parents; Alexandra Ivey, obviously; my Manchester mates; and Giles Foden for opening the door and Robin Robertson for closing it until I was ready.